The Nefarious
By Mia Collins
Chapter One

    Tabitha had reached a place in her life where things were settled but this gave her a strange mixture of relief and sadness as each word was a weight from her shoulders as her words were consumed into the paper by her letting it go. "Goodbye," she murmured, the words now escaping her lips there was relief. It was like gathering a kindling of words to let go and burn once and for all. Even though she had told stories before there was more to tell, and her memories associated with this darkness were free now. But just when she thought all the memories had returned, until the sudden blow of one of the saddest events England had ever faced came to the surface, she realised there was a lot more to come. A lot more suppressed trauma she had to deal with even still, when does it end. She just knew she had to let it go like an unwanted embrace. There were strong memories, little pieces tapering through here and there not making any sense at first but piecing it together one recall at time shuffling it as best she could into order. At first she thought this one day of events were separate occasions but soon began to realise this was the same long day and night flowing into the next morning, probably twenty-four hrs long. But the embers were glowing within her mind as she tried to turn away from the metaphorical fire that had laid dormant as smoke for many years and was now reigniting with a fury, a reminder that some things must be let go. She took a deep breath, leaned back into her armchair and continued to tell her story.

    The three of them pull up in the car park where Tabitha lived. This was a private gravel shared area for the residents who lived in the countryside cottage, there was also a acre or two of land for them all but Tabitha didn't have any need for that and was content with her little gardens front and back, plus she hated gardening. This was a beautiful period red brick cottage with low ceilings, quarry tile floors and two bedrooms where she had her two children, a three year old boy and a baby girl. This row of cottages consisted of six houses that were once three, converted by greed to house more in modern times. They kept the older style of the buildings, nevertheless with their characteristics being cosy historic farm cottages. There were corn fields nearby that Tabitha used to grab the odd few for making popcorn as a youth. At night the sky was inky black because there were no street lights anywhere, it was very peaceful overall and significantly a beautiful place to live.

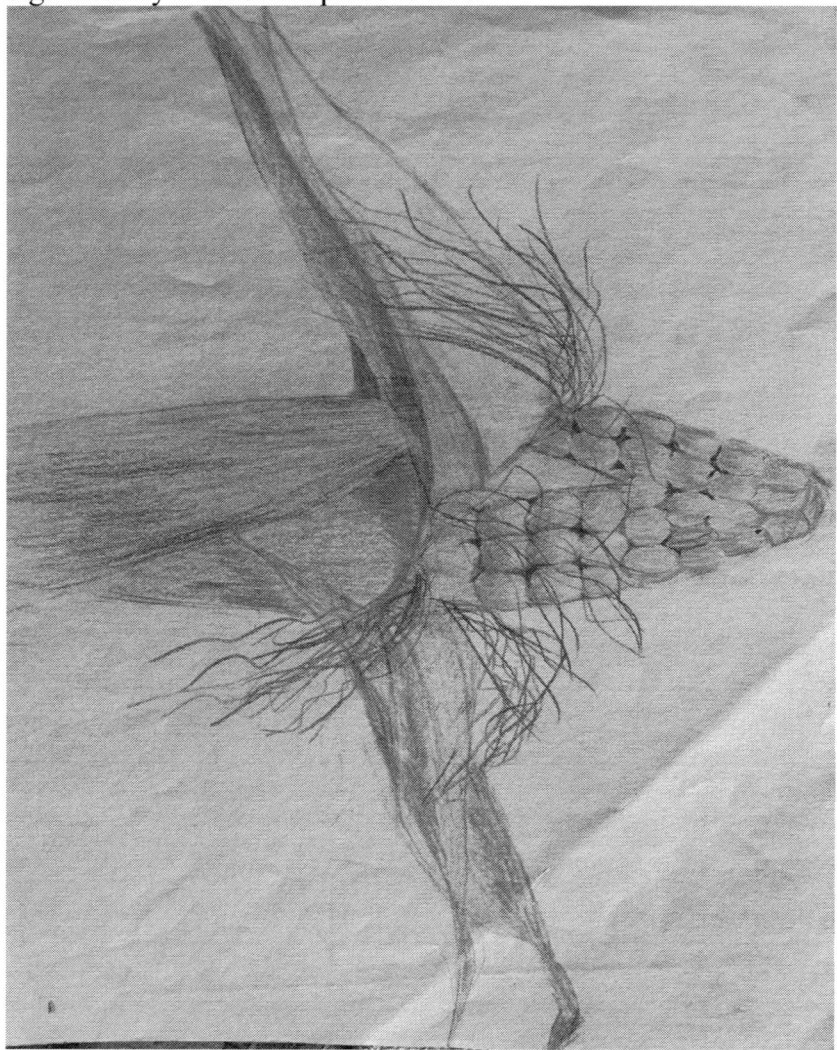

The Golden Cob

As the bodyguard, Shane, is driving, he pulls into the space, they all get out and he throws the keys up in the air for her to catch the mood he was in was upbeat as they had been listening to music on the way home. He was very tall, overweight and had a round face, always smiling a grin that was up to something sinister, deep within his mind pure evil lurked. He had fair short cropped hair. When he spoke he sounded like he was putting on a stupid american accent, it never sounded real. He was always aloof waiting for orders as he didn't have much of a mentality to make decisions alone it seemed. There must have been fragments of his life he must no longer recognise where he drifted so wrongly. It was like he had flames leaping within him where he was never still or happy deep down. This spilled out into his tormenting others' attitude, his cruel fathers words and violence must have echoed into his mind after his passing for him to become so bitterly twisted into a shell copy of him instead of becoming the opposite he became worse feeling a sense of liberation wash over him whenever he was cruel to women and children, he was the monster of all monsters but there was no reasoning because of his lacking of intelligence to make better life choices. He would only damage himself in the very end to live this way but he wasn't self aware enough to realise, and Jonny used him like a puppet and took advantage of his thick braun manipulating him more often than not.

 He walked around the passenger side and took the toy dog out the baby seat that was in the front. Ordering Tabitha he spouts " throw this thing out," she quickly grabs it thinking he is mad, "no that's my baby's favorite toy" grabbing it from him and hugging it close. She placed it in the back seat where the Jonny Stepp and her were sitting for the road trip. The morning was sunny and warm, she was perplexed in addition to feeling a little giddy wondering why the trip was so short.

Jonny

Jonny was a small slim build wiry man, no particular shape to him and tiny features, apart from his big nose that dominated his face at the wrong angle and his often drawn on brows. He had a few accents he would switch from English to an odd American attempt lingo but it never sounded right, could be English farmer to twang and it changed depending who he was talking to at that time. He sometimes wore lifts in his shoes to bring his height up, he had an inferiority complex about his lack of height so he wore quite a lot of makeup, always doing his hair, so he wouldn't leave the house without a hat if his hair wasn't washed, incredibly vain I guess. Jonny was often painting so you'd also see him around the village with paint covered boots. He would go from looking like a tramp to wearing a suit that looked like his older bigger brother had passed down to him, it would hang loose and long with his trousers waist too high. He looked better on TV than real life.

Unbeknown to her Tabitha had been roofied the day before the trip had begun,'Deja vu' in addition to this all she could recall was the last ten mins. How does a roofie work you may think, well, put it this way; if you ever watched a goldfish swim around a bowl and by the time it's done it is forgotten so it will repeat it without getting bored, apparently anyway. This is about the only metaphor one can describe how being stupefied feels, you could be in a club having a great night and by time you get down the road you forget you've just been there and anything that happened. By the time you wake up from a sleep you're a blank canvas from the minute you had it slipped in your drink. You get the jist. Any questions of events will be absolutely nothing to recall. This can also put you into a 'deep unconscious state' depending how much and substance used, but Tabitha was still learning what the street names were as she knew nothing about drugs, only the things you see on Television. She would have this memory of Jonny, he was always barefoot when indoors, something you couldn't help but notice, she thought he had hobbit feet, and even they were covered in tattoos as the years went by, thus became addicted to stamping himself with art, his story of love and pain searching for something he would never find answer to by murdering people.

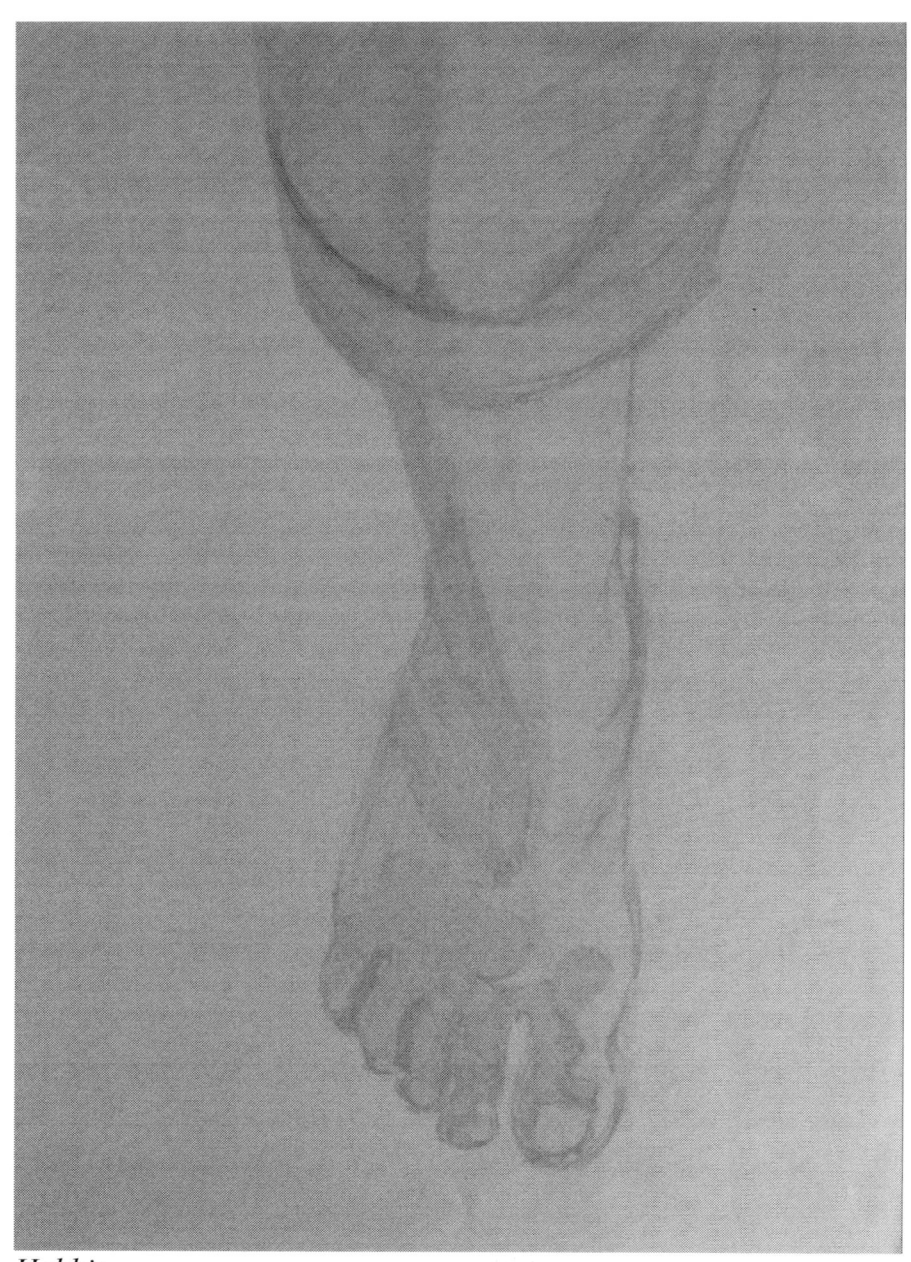
Hobbit

Tabitha
~*The eve of events.*~

Twenty-four hrs before: Jonny approached Tabitha in her back garden, her cottage was located in a small area with a long gravel path with a little lawn going down either side of the path, leading to a picket fence gate that led to the car park. This was so picturesque being hidden from the main road so you wouldn't see any vehicles there apart from the residents. As he was a fairly close neighbour, there were a few houses there he had local and Tabitha had been inside every single one over the years. Jonny had a mansion three doors down with a field gap in between, so why he came to her that day she

Tabitha's Cottage

wasn't sure but he had gotten this idea he wanted to pop to London to see his friend Odie who was born into a billionaire family, although he was not English. She hadn't met Odie before this day either, but often traveled with Jonny meeting new faces all the time so this didn't hinder her. Not only that unbeknown to her she was roofied from the get go, it took her a long time to remember the events later down the line; but we will get to that part soon. She was too entrusting in this man, it wasn't long before the three of them jump in the car, the bodyguard becomes driver, and Tabitha with the celebrity 'actor' sit in the back of this tiny little Fiat beige in colour, there was some damage to it she was repairing at the time she had already undercoated the wing and bonnet in a white primer over black replacement parts, and hadn't got round to the finish coat which would be beige. She wanted it to dry for a couple days first. Jonny pulls out some drinks in the back seat, handing one to her. The mood was upbeat and the three of them were having fun joking around all the way to see Odie. Unbeknown to her he must have slipped a roofie in it, as there was a lot of drifting in and out of knowing where she was. The sun had barely peeked through when they left hers, the boot was packed with her baby's buggy and odd bits for the children, toys, blankets and what not. As they hit the open road the breeze hits her face from the front window she wakes up and for a while they have a carefree spirit of laughter, with a favorite playlist on the cd player. It was as if Jonny had been counting down the days to break free and go out, a burden of work and finally getting a break. They didn't have time for grabbing snacks but Jonny had some beers prepared. As they drove through the rugged countryside with the windows down now living a carefree day in their youth. First stop was fuel, Jonny filled the tank and Tabitha wondered why he needed so much or where they were headed yet. Tabitha and Jonny exchanged glances, each silently acknowledging the moment of untethered freedom; it felt like she was floating on her back looking up at the sky through the rear car window. With beers they salute and enjoy the drive. They arrive in London, manic traffic and tall buildings, lots of beeping vehicles, and taxis galore, this wasn't Tabitha's idea of anything but hell, as a passenger she was fine, but driving in London she hated with a passion. Jonny leads her into the biggest owned store in London, he walks her in on his arm invitingly, he had chuckled in the car after taking a swig then holding his beer like a trophy. Conversions grew deep on the way there but something changed as they arrived, but a comfortable silence fell between them as she felt an overwhelming sense of gratitude for this day out. This store was bigger than Tiffany's as far as names go. The billionaire owner was standing by the lift. He was an older gentleman, he had a kind smile, he

To London

wore a suit, looking the part but he was humble and soft spoken. He said to wait a moment, as he checked the path was clear, down from the lift came the Royal Princess who wore elegant clothing which made her stand out from the crowd. She dressed respectfully, her hair was a lovely shade of golden blond and her looks were stunning, and biggest blue eyes. As she left the lift her bodyguard greeted her and they left the store. At that moment the owner waved his arm to guide them as if to enter the lift, and headed on up to meet with his son Odie. As they exit, upstairs they go out of the lift to the right, then sharp left, there are glass doors leading into a grand living room filled with luxurious furniture with shimmering decor all around. Odie walked over welcoming her, shook her hand and was talking to Jonny . She was handed a drink and sat in a chair. She must have passed out. There was a slight recall of being naked, they must have undressed her while unconscious, Odie walked her towards the bedroom, she looked down "i'm naked," feeling very dizzy, " yes," Odie said "and very nice too" while laughing. He stopped by the window "if you say a word i'll throw you out, look how high it is! " Jonny standing there watching all this while enjoying a smoke while he waited his turn laughed you sick bastard, he turned heel and took her to a different spot to rape in the living room, but he didn't want Jonny watching him so he walked her back into his bedroom laying her on the bed before running back to close the big door behind so they had privacy. He bragged " you won't get better than this room for luxury." All of a sudden he dropped the hard act and became loving, kissing and caressing all over Tabitha's body. He was putty in her hands, but she didn't want him; she just knew if she tried to fight it Jonny would beat her again. He suddenly got up from the bed of foreplay, and ran to the bathroom running a bubble bath, he then came back took Tabitha by the hand and led her telling her to climb in, he stepped in joining her, swiftly rolled her on top of himself while caressing her breasts sliding his hands all the way over her body exploring every inch. The bath had deep sides and you lay any end, he wanted to finish up on the bed, he made her stand wrapped a towel around her but just before because she had noticed the garden through the window he led her out to the patio area on the roof to show her how luxury his place was with a smile. "Look it goes all the way back to there" pointing, then led her back inside. It was like he was showing her around why he was suddenly being nice now after the harsh intro in front of Jonny, or was that just a show. She woke up with wet hair on his bed laying on clean towels and Jonny was standing over her. This time he had his back turned, as he turned around he smiled and said; "told you I'd bring you into luxury", she had already forgotten the bath and Odie. After it was over, she woke up sometime later again this time with Odies father shaking her shoulder and asking her if she was ok, she was now dressed sitting in an armchair in the living room, whether she did that herself or they did she was still unsure. She had no idea how long she was unconscious. Furthermore, she believes she was in that apartment a lot longer than mentioned by Jonny. Were these men in the same boat as Jonny with his dark underworld, involved in this trafficking rig? It was clear he was digging his own grave, but he wasn't aware yet and nor was Tabitha on this day. He had no idea his loose end was his bodyguard telling all when he had a few drinks he'd let things slip, he did so with a patronizing look on his face, a smirk you could say, believing 'she won't remember any of this.' As they headed out toward the lift to leave, Jonny remarked; "I'm going to have to give you some coke," Tabitha firmly refused as they walked into the lift hallway area. "Wait here!" He runs back into the living room passing through the glass doors and grabs her a bottle of beer, opens it with his back turned, shakes it and passes it to her, at which it goes all over the plush carpet next to the lift. Odie comes around the corner as they enter the lift, he stands there then looks down and sees the puddle of beer on the floor, he shouts at Tabitha about how expensive the carpet is, her reaction considering she was feeling dizzy she managed to point to Jonny " it's his fault he shook my drink," then the two men smiled as perhaps Odie realised what Jonny had slipped a drug into it, but Tabitha was unaware until she started to chat a lot more than usual with a high energy effect. She even at this point still unaware of being raped upstairs. She didn't choose this; it was all forced upon her.

 Jonny and Tabitha go back down in the lift together, as they step out the owner is stood waiting again to let them know the coast is clear to leave without prying eyes of the public, the lift goes back up and Odie follows down in it, as he exits " Jonny why don't you two join us for a night out in Paris ?" Jonny suddenly excited; "really? France but we don't have our passports on us,"" it's fine stay close to us we will get you in and out,"responded Odie. That was it, the decision was made, "we're off to France girl" Jonny chuckled, with a sound of utter excitement in his voice, he quickly added to Odie "but can I bring my bodyguard he's outside waiting ?"

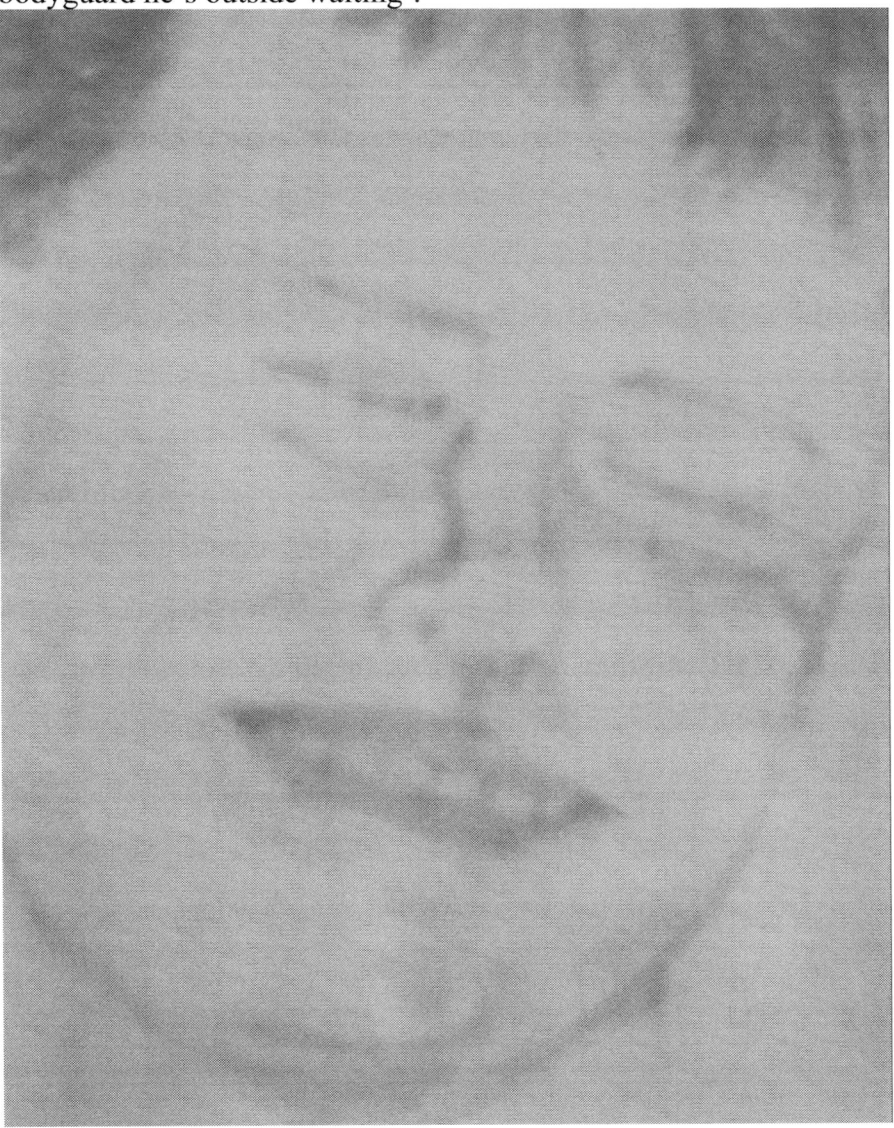

Jonny's bodyguard

　The nod was given by Odie, "of course let's go." but the weight of expectations had begun heavily on her mind, so the night still had surprises in store, she should be feeling an overwhelming gratitude but some gut feeling was screaming something sinister was on the cards. Jonny tried to comfort her, "don't worry this will be a wonderful adventure for us both just relax." They all agreed to meet at a certain time and the fiat would follow their car into France. Afterthought, Odie only invited them because of Tabitha, this wasn't for Jonny this was to impress her, he had a soft spot and she felt it, he had warmed to her after the bath together he had let down his hard man act.   They headed back to the village and once they arrived back at Tabitha's cottage they had a short window of time to get ready and shoot back to meet them. She needed to do her makeup, rushing so she was ready in time. Nevertheless spirits were high for Jonny , he walked in wearing trousers and a shirt tucked in asking her approval. "What do you think? Do I look smart enough?" He was more excited than her.. "Yeah you look good" she replied, giving him the once over. The three of them hurry into the car and head out to a meeting place of the two cars where agreed. Now heading for the tunnel. Along the way Jonny and her reminisce about their younger days until she passes out again.

Present time: __ Tabitha was unable to recall just yet all of it; there are still a lot of missing gaps in her memory, but she knows by now to trust the process, over the years she'd had so many returned memories that she had found photos and proof of events so she knew she was on the right track. The question was, what's she gonna do about it?__

The right thing of course there is no other choice but to put things right for the royal family, who she had met members of years before, at the end of the day they have love for one another the same as any other family, life has its ups and downs but it doesn't mean you stop loving them. She had recently been reading on the internet about the Passing of the Princess in a car accident and how heartbroken the world was upon hearing this, and the tears shed by the royals.

Odies Bodyguard

Jonny was off the chain with his inability to be a gentle human being.

Day after accident: Tabitha had been driving over the half penny bridge on her way to get fuel, the same day she heard the announcement over the radio, she had a lot of errands to run and swore she had filled the tank a day ago, but her needle was on empty so she was heading for the nearest garage. The news shocked her to the core, she had to pull over and turn the radio up. How horribly sad. Unbeknown she had zero recollection of the day before. Tabitha had no idea she must have gone inside, nodded off for a couple hrs and woken up and thought the day was new. Often with these events she would miss days and get days muddled up and now it all makes sense in hindsight, but now it was too little too late unfortunately. She remembers being in a busy atmosphere it felt like a bar but in fact it was the Ritzy in France, she was sitting next to Princess Mary-Rose on a bench seat with a table in the middle of them all, the music was loud and the place was packed, sitting adjacent to her was her boyfriend Odie, Princess Mary-Rose leaned across with her arm stretched out beside her leaning her head in close because the music was very loud talking to Tabitha she asked what do you think of my new boyfriend? Tabitha Replying, "lovely, yes and he seems smitten with you." He looks like he's in love; he hasn't taken his eyes off you. This made the princess smile, she then leaned over to Odie and told him what she said, he gave her the nod of approval and smiled but he had a look of guilt in his eye, although Tabitha had already forgotten earlier that day. He smiled at her remark and they both laughed. Their mood was upbeat; he wasn't looking at any other women but the Princess which made him appear more charming. Shortly after while the Princess left her seat to go to the ladies, Odie leaned over and said something, it was muffled because of the loud music but it was something like "don't say anything about back at the apartment," she had no idea what he meant, or maybe he meant the roofie he'd seen Jonny give her in the beer, maybe something happened while she was unconscious, alas she had no recall in that moment so his comment went over a deaf ear. He leans forward a second time they're alone " Your eyes are stunning" she didn't know how to respond to it so just said thank you and looked away, a little embarrassed. Tabitha was uncertain about Odie's meaning 'please don't say anything,' but she began to experience faint memories from that day in his apartment. She felt that there was more to uncover regarding her experience after being roofied by Jonny on that day. Something happened alright. __It was clear Tabitha was having difficulty recalling yet all the night's conversation but she was sure it would come back to her nevertheless. The men were drinking beers matching the joy they all seemed to be feeling in that moment in the bar that evening, Tabitha had one drink as far as she recalls but every time she went to the ladies she was escorted by Jonny's bodyguard Shane, this night he was on his best behaviour acting like he should, not like he did on other occasions where he'd been atrocious. Scrap that; Spoke too soon Unfortunately it didn't last long, he was a brute toward the end. She turned to the Princess who was sitting to the right of her at the table to ask "why does that bodyguard keep following me everywhere?"

Moments
The Princess laughed but Tabitha was being serious and didn't get the joke. He was really annoying her. She supposed the Princess was used to it by now but Tabitha was a free spirit and hated someone in her pocket. Tabitha had no idea that the public could be so dangerous that she would need him by her side. Little did she know the one to be afraid of was the brute all along, talking about wolves in sheep's

clothing but that is now history. The music was blasting in there setting the tone to up beat in their spirits of joy. Everyone was having a nice time. Apart from the annoying bodyguard following Tabitha around. She would have happily swapped bodyguards as the princesses one was a lot nicer. But she didn't need one; she'd kept her head in the shadows all this time even when with Jonny they had a way of hiding her. The evening went fast but this could be because there is a lot more yet to come for the memory bank, it was time for suppressed memories to give it up and let her see it. It wasn't long before Odie and Tabitha had a disagreement, he shouted over the loud music "if you tell the Princess what happened I will have you killed. Do you know who I am and what I'm capable of?" She snapped back at him "don't you dare threaten me" with angry eyes daggering deep into his soul. This had him taken back that she wasn't afraid of him, when the princess came back from the ladies, she leaned in and told her "he just threatened to kill me if I were you i'd think hard about considering if you accept his proposal or not." but she didnt mention the rape because she had already forgotten it. This caused a row between the couple Odie leaning in grovelling as hard as he could to win her back and waved a sorry to Tabitha. He knew at this point he couldn't intimidate her. She'd been through this sorta thing her entire life with Jonny and there comes a point you're just used to it. Jonny had followed her into the ladies, grabbed her chest hard and slammed her into the cubical bashing her through the doors, a moment before he'd told his bodyguard to watch nobody comes in and catches him, he then proceeds to repeatedly punch her in her stomach a place nobody could see the bruises under her clothing this was something he had practice in clearly. After Jonny left slamming the door behind him and yelling angrily at her she had no idea why, then a lady came out the cubicle she had overheard the fight, but she didn't speak English so couldn't understand Tabitha saying "I've just been beaten up" holding her stomach in pain, the women shrugged as if to say sorry and left. As Tabitha walks out the driver this time was standing outside the door saying "you've had enough don't drink no more," but she only had one, so the drug slipped in her glass was noticeable to others but they presumed drink which was not the case, she had no money or purse she was there on the shirt tails of Odie and the princess, not really Jonny he wasn't helping only hindering, abusing. In actual fact he was a human trafficker but she wasn't aware in the early years what that meant. This doesn't always mean you vanish for good, it can mean they come and go in your life, drug you and take you, dump you and you never remember a single thing, so be open minded how traffickers work, it can come in the form of grooming for many decades. After the fight she then went back to the booth seat and apologised to the princess's bodyguard who was standing to 'her' left or right looking in.. Tabitha said she was leaving and he agreed to pass on the msg for her goodbye. The princess waved and Tabitha waved a sorry sign back holding her bruised tummy. This spurred everyone at this point to call it a night. Aggressive men, abusers Tabitha was in the hands of now. Little did anyone know she had just been beaten and all because she had disagreed with something Odie had said. Tabitha told him what she thought of him. She became very honest after he tried to control her, which upset him. She couldn't tell anymore than the present row because she couldn't recall what Odie was talking about that night anyway. From what she told Tabitha she hadn't made up her mind yet, as it was too soon, she was wise to not jump in yet. She was way too good for him was all she knew. This had a knock on effect where Jonny beat her in the ladies, additionally Odie had a lot of groveling to do with the Princess. Only problem was Tabitha had forgotten the argument five min later. When they all stood to leave the bar, at first they walked past a lot of stairs, the hotel was designed in Louis XVI style an all time masterpiece of architecture compared to the royal palace with its grand vistas, lofty proportions and sparkling chandeliers which were distracting Tabitha as she walked through, Jonny hurrying her up but she was admiring all its beauty and wasn't quick enough for him as usual. Just ahead the Princess with her team walked into the lift. But Tabitha was still admiring the surroundings to keep up with any of them.

King
The hallways were plush with grand patterned carpets and fancy wall trimmings including grand mirrors along the walls that reflected the lights perfectly, in elegant taste, lots of gold detailing on railings and walls, including the crown mouldings which gave a finishing touch of luxury no matter where your eyes looked every inch was grandly

finished. The glamor was an all time masterpiece she wasn't going to see again and she wanted to take it all in. The place was elignat with impeccable service; she had noticed others being waited on hand and foot. But she was also surprised unofficially how they're lives were kinda normal too, the freedom the princess had to wander around with Odie and the bodyguard hanging back on his phone like it's all fine i'm right here so casual. It was about as grand as it gets for Tabitha, well second best her favorite place and memory was inside Buckingham Palace but was in years to come after this as history goes, pinpointing time and place. As she walks through the long corridors guided by Jonny she'd already forgotten the beating he just gave her in the ladies while his bodyguard kept anyone entering and stood to look out. She looked at him and said " remember when we thought we'd be rock stars by now ?" He wasn't listening, he was watching ahead where to go following Odie and company. They all briefly go upstairs to the Princesses room, she tells all the men to stay by the door and asks Tabitha to follow her quickly they go through the suite turning left into a bathroom en suite. Suddenly she asks "now tell me quickly we don't have a lot of time what's going on?" She was concerned for Tabitha's well being and explained "I can help if you tell me?" I'm a member of the Royal Family, "I demand you tell me everything that has happened tonight, I can help you." She had the phone with her incase she needed to call for help. Unfortunately Tabitha couldn't, the roofie had taken its toll on her thoughts, moments later Odie came barging in to demand what was so private, he was most likely worried she'd tell on what he did to her that day, but Tabitha didn't remember ten minutes ago let alone that day. They all then left heading back towards the lifts, Tabitha and Jonny walked a bit further back then the others, so he could give her more telling off away from prying ears. When they all enter the lift was when Jonny convinces them to head back to England, in fact he insisted rudely in reality going on about he had work the next day so he selfishly changed the course of history because of his insistence. Odies driver Paulo speaks up. "I don't mind driving. I feel fine if you like to," but he had been downing beers in the bar at high speed thinking he wasn't driving, __only they hadn't hit him yet. It's the fresh air that hits you after a drink. They agree and then head off and walk in opposite directions, Odie's group to the back and Jonny's to the front, Tabitha finds herself walking through a room with glamorous sofas, moments before she had to pass the two bodyguards chatting by a doorway she cowered crossing her arms in fear as Jonny's bodyguard had too threatened her just before, he put on a fake smile and waved her through in front of the Odie's bodyguard to not let his real self be caught out. But if he worked for Odie perhaps he already knew what went on behind closed doors, he seemed so nice so hoped he wasn't the same. They pass through an impressive room nevertheless, a lobby perhaps or a communal room for guests, she noticed the cameras and so did Jonny, so he insisted they walk separately to not be caught out together. Then Jonny suddenly realises they're going the wrong way and turns heel to change route, heading back toward the front exit, as the Princess and Odie headed out the back they carried on their path. "Please, hold on," she whispered, Tabitha's determination palpable as she was trying to find her bearings of the room and direction Jonny was pointing her to. It was easy to get lost inside the most famous Hotel in Paris. The three head out the front then walk through the entrance, exiting toward Tabitha's old banger that Shane had already collected and driven right up close for them to hop in quickly so Jonny can hide from the press. It looked kinda silly sitting there next to a row of stylish billionaire cars waiting. Jonny nods for her to get in, she climbs in after him they sit in the back due to a baby seat and a toy dog with a mussel on its nose, its a cute toy that her baby loved, this made her laugh actually with the large bodyguard driving sat next to this toy being so the opposite of him, he was the butt of her jokes all the way when she awake. Just as the drive away from hotel Jonny gives Tabitha a punch in the face with "there you go, don't need to hide your bruises now do we, so behave." She was so drowsy she didn't react at all, just leaned back silent. By the time they got through town the mood was upbeat, the radio was switched on and they headed off. Jonny pipes up: "turn it down man we need to find the river, they said follow the river and I need to concentrate," so the radio knob was twisted down to a low setting. As they follow the river Jonny says "look up at the sky" and points out the stars were dotting the sky like diamonds. The peace before the storm, this would be in hindsight. They left first, so they arrived a little sooner than the Princess, her billionaire boyfriend, the bodyguard and driver, they then sit to wait by the tunnel entrance keeping their eye for their car, as their car passes Jonny shouted "there is Odie, quick catch up man," as he speeds off up behind it they enter the tunnel knowing they have to be with them to get past the customs. Suddenly Jonny shouts ", no, I can't be seen its the press, its the press, "SHIT MAN fuck go, go faster lose

Paulo

Princess Mary-Rose

the fucking bastards, they are right up our ass… get rid of them," at that the Princess's car is now on their left in the two lanes, the driver suddenly tightening of the steering wheel as he veered off to the left sharp and aggressive "fuck" he raws,Tabitha turns around in the back seat and gets a good look at the press on their peds and they get a good look at her, she can seel the flashes of cameras and it's blinding.

Tabitha reached and clicked her seatbelt in and told Jonny to do the same, he unclicked her belt with fierce determination in his gaze "no, you can fucking die too" his voice strong yet trembling, one min he's nice then nasty. Suddenly Jonny's bodyguard turned the wheel banging into them, well it felt like that but suppose when he swerved over their lane they were trying to pass on the left and hit the rear light then the front wing as well. He thinks it's the press on their mopeds but it's the Princess, "shit" Shane gasps, as they panic and hit the speed to get away from our car wondering what he's playing at, the royal driver had a few drinks in him too so he could be in real trouble. The Bodyguard James, waving at Shane to get back with a angry look on his face, while the driver was red faced livid with rage, in that moment ordered by the princess to cruze beside Tabitha's car momentarily, so he held back while the princess waved a concerned face and hand gesture palm up fingers wide spread at Tabitha "are you ok, are you ok, are you ok?" compelling her to speak up as Jonny was squeezing her knee while telling her under his breath "don't say a word," Tabitha waved "I'm ok and smiled, but she felt out of it. She was wobbling around in the back like she was about to pass out from shock. "Stop! Don't say anything more! Jonny shouted. Unknowingly holding their breath for what was to come. Over the princesses shoulder Odie was pointing to his cheek then Tabithas asking how did she get that mark he looked angry at Jonny , he knew. The princess smiled but looked concerned for Tabitha before exclaiming to her driver he can now go, this was the moment he raced ahead grinding the first gear as he did so the Mary-Rose shouted out to him calm down Paulo waving her hand toward his shoulder to tell him to go steady, but in a furious red faced temper then slipping it into a low gear and sped off at an incredibly high speed before plugging into darkness they vanished ahead out of sight.

Earlier in the bar: Tabitha overheard their driver say "well I'm not driving for the first time in weeks so I'm going to see how many I can have in two hrs."__ "How many do you think you can do man?" asked Jonny; at that the driver downs a pint real fast while the men stood around him and laughed.

There was then a cacophony: a screeching of tyres filled the air followed by a loud crash, Tabitha froze her heart pounding. As they arrived at the scene through the right lane their car was a stark contrast against the twisted metal of the vehicle. While their lives hang in the balance, there was a faint smell of blood and exhaust fumes. The suspense of heart pounding tethering on a mix of fear and concern. Their car had span 360` they had no choice but to go into the left lane circumventing the merc, Shane was rubbernecking the injured, then he pulled to a standstill alongside looking directly into the car. The lights still flashing and alarm beeps as if to cry for help like a flare gun at sea. Cutting through the panic Jonny was still commanding as if it was nothing but an inconvenience, he had a calm demeanor about him. As they past conscientiously, theres a wheel in the road that came off, "the Princess is alive, shes alive good" quietly spoken by Jonny, "lets go man let the fucking press deal with it. They did this!" Tabitha looks at Odie laying there motionless, and wonders to herself for a moment if he is alive, is he breathing; "ODIE!" __ " shush," Jonny whispers "shut the fuck up." The Princess hear's her turns and looks right at Tabitha beckoning with her hand and asks "help us help us!" Tabitha nods ok pointing to where they will park up. Shane pulls the car forward responding "Tabitha shouts through the back window, we're just going to pull up over here and I'll help you ok, " the Princess nods "ok thank you." While Tabitha is executing them to stop Jonny orders Shane to go "fuck them" he shouts, "drive." Tabitha shouts "no, go back, go back, she needs our help," but Jonny didn't have any remorse in his body. What had happened to him, who he is now, it's like he's become his own evil alter ego, where was the kindness inside him, or was the nice guy just always an act? Well that's what it appears to be.

    Just before the crash and first impact with the fiat; breaking her rear left light and front left wing became loose with a long scratch down it. Tabitha looks behind and there were loads of motorcycles, she responds; "it's bikes." she was fascinated by the scooters and the doubled up riders with the pillion holding the cameras now that was impressive, she was mad for bikes in her youth so this seemed exciting she was also conscientious of bikers as being one herself she knew how to tread carefully around them and let them pass when needed, bikers always recognised the code and other bikers would know a fellow biker by how they drive. Jonny then orders her to not look back and duck down to ensure the press do not spot her. Of course he didn't. She now had a black eye on her left side of her face from when he punched her back at the start when they first jumped in the back seat together. He grabs her neck and pushes her head down behind the driver's seat firmly while he's trying to hide at the same time. That's the moment it all went wrong as 'the swerve was meant for the bikes.' Tabitha was perplexed at the bikers and began to count them, pointing to focus she got to eight she thinks before Jonny pushed her head down again in temper. She noticed one of them was a woman. She tried to do up her seat belt again and Jonny stopped her, angry that she'd try. He was showing all signs of narcissism but she wasn't in a relationship so why was he like this with her? That's what men do with women they're close to, and half the time she couldn't remember his name because he spiked so much over the years she just kept forgetting him, or was that what made him so mad, there is no explanation.

Shane stops the car alongside the crash, they all look in, Tabitha was unable to focus at first but tries hard to see and understand what she's looking at, the drug they put in her drink was making it hard to feel anything, it stops rational thought processing. It didn't help that he spiked her uppers and downers. Tabitha looks at everyone. Odie is laying head facing away on the driver's left hand side seat which has crushed the driver through the steering wheel with his head covered heavily in blood, so much so she could no longer see his features. Odie isn't moving, his head looks injured, she presumed dead because he is motionless, without checking the pulse she couldn't be entirely sure. The driver lifts his head and turns it to face the princess, at which the princess calls out his name in pure empathy being shocked to her core, Tabithas having difficulty recognising him for his injuries and blood soaked face. The steering wheel was non-existent to be seen, gone into pieces as his chest was forced into it. He lifts up his head then his head drops, as he tries to lift it one more time it drops again and in that moment she thinks he's now gone. Tabitha just witnessed a man die in front of her eyes. She could do nothing but stare in shock, her body froze unable to move or react. Odies bodyguard James is in the passenger seat, it is not as far forward as the drivers but it has shifted, his face is dripping with blood but he's unconscious, then his eyes flutter open momentarily filled with confusion and fear. He had deep face lacerations not as bad as the driver though. Before his eyes rolled back unconscious once more she could see him breathing and felt a sigh of relief. It felt like she was dreaming floating, almost trying to understand her surroundings. The Princess was moving and alert but clearly she was in agony holding her chest. The woman who she had been laughing with seeing now suddenly like this was difficult to comprehend. Emotions were muffled but they stirred deep inside, like the beginning of the burial of trauma had begun. Then ruthlessly Johnny ordered the driver to go. What would benefit him more if he could get away with running he would. The roofie Tabitha was being spiked with was confusing her, they drive along the tunnel a while they pull over, stop and park up on the right, there is no traffic yet but Jonny and Shane were discussing trying to figure out a flawless plan how to get out the other end with the cameras on the exit considering what just happened, to hide himself. Jonny then hushes Tabitha while he was on the phone putting on a funny accent she thinks calling an ambulance. Why he couldn't be honest but his entire life was a lie. Time seemed to stretch as they waited so long she fell asleep again, not for want of trying to stay awake but the roofie took control. She tried once more to tell them to go back and help but Jonny feared his identity would be found out.

She had this feeling they may have not just roofied her but roofied the other car passengers as well but that's just hindsight she has no evidence on this, but she wouldn't put it past Jonny and Shane to do something so low . The more she recalls she does remember the other driver downing pints, Jonny had filled the table with many drinks. In the presence she feels a mix of feelings anger and sorrow about Odie, how dare he do that to her at his apartment, and how dare he try to be seductive at the hotel while he was sat with his beautiful girlfriend who Tabitha liked, she would never of slept with anyones man, she only wanted a loyal man herself after all so this was horrifying to be forced into that situation. So many emotions are trying to bubble to surface, anger and sadness as she wouldn't want to see them dead, now all she sees is the last moments flashing over and over of them looking through the car window at her asking her if she is ok with concern, they showed her concern then they crash moments later. This was too much to process. She needs to recall why they rowed at the bar, what did she say that got Odie into a mood, it doesn't take much for her to upset someone she had no filter. But that part isn't back just yet. He did apologise; she recalls that much at least.

She must have passed out, as she awakes and sees an odd looking ambulance fly past, this was when Jonny had another plan up his sleeve to try and set Tabitha up to look like the driver. The fact is the press already knew she was innocent. He spent his entire life living a lie so another didn't matter to him. The two men discuss that they better go back and come up with some fabricated story of events. Jonny and Tabitha walk back up to the crash, the tone of their adventure was dropped. leaving the driver in the car he stays behind paranoid and over the limit. Shane had once told her when Jonny couldn't hear that he didn't want to do these things to her but Jonny forced him with blackmail of setting him up, grassing his crimes as a lure to use him like a puppet. He tried to pass the buck to Jonny but they were as bad as each other, one a sociopath the other a psychopath she thought in hindsight. All these labels would flow in her mind about them but she wasn't qualified to pick one but they had traits of all. While standing at the crash scene they just approached on foot. A tall man with a receding hairline, a doctor perhaps, approaches Tabitha, he speaks in English, are you the driver ? "No" she responds. "I was in the back seat," he looked confused, she pointed back to the car "back there in the car he's the driver," she's just being honest but feeling very uneasy on her feet. She was only relaxed about it if that makes sense no guilt because she knows shes telling the truth, to lie about something so serious there would be no calmness about it, what was Jonny doing lying, does he not realise he will be caught out eventually, it's easier to own up than keep going through life with insanity which she has realised now that's what's up with him. She realises there is no empathy in him whatsoever. The doctor had approached her once more in the chaos of the emergency responders. He had a calm demeanor about him, in the face of calamity, he was calm considering the weight of the lives hanging in the balance. While they worked on the Princess he was examining Tabitha's pulses in her wrists he explained you're very calm, yes she responded why wouldn't I be, she already didn't remember the crash or where she was. The drug took a profound wave over her. Despite thoughts of her mind twirling within her she couldn't make a lot of sense of anything. But she was standing up. She inhaled sharply and focused on the task at hand, trying to understand her surroundings but it was no good. Stay with me she urged softy but he had to go and help the other medical teams at the crash. She went to walk forward as the press wanted a picture of her, then the doctor reaching out touching her arm told her not to look in the car as she passed. The team carefully lifted the Princess onto the stretcher "you're going to be ok" as they tried to calm her__a promise mingled with hope, even as the weight of reality loomed dark and heavy. Tabitha's skin felt cold in fact she felt a cold chill all around her as if she knew already the dead were standing next to her__a one last goodbye. But she brushed off the thoughts with the hope instead they'd be ok but fate loomed heavily on her mind. The paparazzi are taking photos. Everyone had theirs taken for the record. But the copies weren't great. They took a picture of Jonny but somehow he slips through the press of identification,he gives a fake name when asked to identify himself this made Tabitha's eyebrows sharpen into a frown at him, he hushed her with spiteful eyes back. He told her to shut up. But she did not heed the warning. She overheard Jonny threatening one of the press for taking photos, adding "do you know who I am?" He was furious. She can't recall how long the crowd stood around but They headed back to the car which was now seeming invitingly a comfort to her as she still felt funny and dizzy, she was succumbing to the sleepy effect of the roofy. They climb back in the back seat. After all it was an accident or perhaps he knew it was his fault deep down. The bodyguard drives them again, they cruze ahead until they arrive at the end of the tunnel, it's now daylight ahead she can see the exit, finally seeing daylight blindingly bright after spending a night inside a tunnel. It's about fifty yards as they pull over again, they force her to drive from this point,Shane grabs her violently dragging her from the car and orders her to drive. Her shoulder was hurting now and so was her stomach and chest from Jonny's punches earlier in the loo back at the Ritzy. The bright sunlight is blinding her, as she looks back in her mirror the two men have their T Shirts over their faces like "what are you doing?" She laughed, perplexed as to who was in that car that had crashed, confused and stupefied to where she had just been and didn't even know where she was heading back to England. She wasn't with it, she'd lost all ability to reason or question anything. She drove past the camera then she was ordered to stop and swap again, she'd only driven another fifty yards if that. Their plan was avoiding the camera. Selfish, they should have stayed and helped the injured but whatever it was they slipped in her drink made her lose touch with any rational thought process. She had already forgotten by this point they had walked back to the scene of the crash earlier. When they exited the tunnel she overheard Jonny telling Shane, "they will bury Odie tonight because he is a muslim, that's good they won't have time hopefully to find what was in his system." Did they roofie him too? The press had already snapped her in the back seat entering the tunnel. If only she had remembered she would have gone right to the police immediately in fact if she was driving they'd all be alive today. As she recalls it over and over in her mind of the asshole bodyguards road rage. If it had been her driving when he shouted press she would have waved at them and let them pass safely but that's just too normal for their world. All that anger and hatred isn't the way forward in life. The press are simply doing their job the same as anybody else. Yeah maybe they call out abuse to get an awful expression out of them, but let's face it there are a lot of hostile people in the world and Tabitha was realising the press weren't so bad if she compared them to some celebrities, maybe they know they deserved it who knows. She had just met the most wonderful people she ever could meet in a lifetime yet to be invited was an honor she will never get again in this lifetime or by anyone so kind hearted. How can these men live with themselves with what they have done? As the years passed to make things worse Jonny paid a random man who wanted a buck or two to fabricate a story that it was him in his car, including they created a story about painting the car and they even made up the dog was real when it was a toy. Honestly is it because he had contacts in the press he gotta make this rubbish up. This is perjury, this is vile, this is criminal. All she knew was the Royals were about the best bet as far as honour could stretch, she knew she could trust the King and his family meaning on account of her meeting was brief but how they were and treated her was about as close to a perfect gentleman could be. The way all men should be but let's face it that will not happen. As the weeks went past she decided she no longer wanted the Fiat, not recalling the accident there was no deceit, as a result a couple months later she headed to the local garage to park and exchange it. The car dealer opened up the bonnet and was inspecting the left wing. In the back seat were some old guitar picks Jonny had given her along the way apart from that she'd cleaned it out. He looked at her as he spurted out "have you killed someone with this?" Tabitha laughed, "What, are you insane?" She thought he has an odd sense of humour, so digressed back to the sales conversation "what cars do you have she asked?" He looked at her again. Have you seen the news? She must have appeared lost, he added "a car like this is being looked for by the police;" she blurted up " well it's not me,"

his response was now becoming weird "are you sure you haven't been to france in it?" Tabitha
Just laughed at what else she could do. He was creepy like most men who run garages. She found they're always so dishonest and wanted to leave as soon as possible. " Besides, the car was shimmering with new paint as she had sprayed it herself and wondering why he didn't shut up and do the deal as she was about to leave. I've never been to France!" but at this point in her life she hadn't recalled all the times she had been there due to being trafficked and roofied __ her life flowed and somehow she kept moving forward oblivious to her black outs, in fact she thought life was great. Not knowing is probably better in one sense. Ignorance is bliss and the unknowing is even better! When one remembers these things you can't just let it be and say oh well let it go, there must be __ vengeance. A week or so after the accident Jonny popped round and took the necklace she wore that he had lent to her, she was confused, she didn't recall borrowing it, that was an odd memory to resurface but brushed it off as meaningless. She recalled even bumping into the bodyguard of the princess ten years after. He was drinking with Jonny, Tabitha was led by the arm across the bar and introduced by Jonny, " you remember this man don't you?" She was confused and shaking her head. She asked him how he got his scars, he never turned to face her, he kept his stance sideways but he crossed over one arm to shake her hand. He told her he didn't remember and don't want to talk about it but mentioned it was a car crash, to which she replied with a pained face "ouch," his eyes then turned to look at her with surprise in them, seeing she was empathetic even though she didn't remember him at that time. Her gaze drifted upward deep in thought, "I guess it would be; metal against flesh, sorry that happened to you," "thank you and yes." That moment was odd but she was still unaware of who he was. It's a strange feeling to recall even those conversations that all piece together like a jigsaw eventually. She didn't stay to talk but one thing for sure by the way he looked at her he remembers more than he was letting on. But to drink with Jonny who basically caused the crash if you were to pan it all right back, was he ever aware he may as well have been drinking with the devil himself, because he definitely was no angel.

  Her life now is decades on and she's having to deal with the day after these horrid events one after the other without much break in

between, PTSD memory gain whatever the technical term maybe. It's a lot to shuffle into its right order, but somehow she's unscathed, her emotional feelings are pushed aside and she's solely focused on making things right for all those hurt in the past. It's not her responsibility but if they are not man enough to stand up and do the right thing she had to. She recalls the conversion with the Prince years later after the crash she had a wonderful night talking to him outside the Palace, and inside, where he in fact asked her where was she when she heard the reports on the news and he said you must be one of the first broadcasts to hear it then, he showed her a photo of the place she was the night she sent her son text letting him know she was ok and where she was. He was deeply saddened and Tabitha will always remember what a lovely man he was. He was genuinely kind hearted like his mother the Princess. With all these memories flooding back she was now piecing together like a jigsaw in her mind. All she knows is she had to do the right thing for everyone even though it was making her own life hell on earth, she was being shut down left right and centre and lost many friends but she wasn't letting this stop her. Losing people no longer mattered. She had thought about it like 'thanks for clearing my war path' so she can now carry on with her mission. All she knew was do the right thing, be honest, keep going, be strong and don't let these fools stand in her way, she would have to learn how to prevail. She could see how easy it was for them to get away with their lies so her faith in the law had dropped dramatically. She was honestly wondering how on earth they passed any exams in criminology at all. She is the first one to run herself down, she doesn't think herself better or more intelligent at all she just knows that it's easy to tell the truth and it's easy to bring up when asked. If you start with lies you'll never keep a story straight. So if you're faced with the law just tell the truth, no matter what it's better to face it right away than later down the line as life will be hell and high water once the world thinks you lied to them. For them to lie to the Royal family is a disgrace!
____*Off with their fk -in heads she thought to herself.*

What could she do at this stage to get the Royals to listen to her, after her conversion with the Prince she felt like he already knew the questions he was asking her that night in the car. She was still unable to recall if she had a Blue Fiat 500 that particular evening or a red

astra, no matter she had too many cars over the years probably one every year due to being old bangers the mot runs out she had to get a new one as they're so old in the early days it worked out better that way. So she was unable to point out the car information, oddly how she recalls some details perfectly clearly but other important things are still lost, the only way she can prove it is the DVLA database for records so she hopes the Royals can access this for themselves once she reaches out and gets to speak to the Royal Investigation team. Or maybe they are finished grieving so she didn't want to bring up old wounds to them, but she thinks someone needs to hear the truth even if it's just for the history records. But one thing is for sure she had to try her absolute best before she threw in the book. She hadn't reported the doctor for what he'd done the day Jonny lured her to his workshop and handed her a bottle of water, then took her into his car with his driver, another abduction on the list of many. She felt like some deserved justice, some would slip through her wrath, but the more blocks he keeps placing in front of her she may need to come out and just tell on him too. She had to start being harder on these men. Not just for her but for all victims, there needs to be a new law in place where everyone gets a fair investigation no matter what.
She was ready to shake the world and watch it rattle.

Twenty seven years pass, one afternoon Tabitha found herself looking in the documentaries to see if anything she recalls was similar making sure her memories were correct and low and behold, she spots herself walking across the screen on CCTV in an investigation; now this is starting to add up, when she had met the Prince years later at the famous london club a mile from the palace he had showed her pictures asking her lots of questions about the shop, the hotel, and her car, questioning what colour was it. Perhaps that meeting with the Royal wasn't such a coincidence after all he had to find out for himself and he did he realised she was innocent due to she had zero recollection of the event, this was still a period of many decades where the roofying affected her life she would lose time lose days when Jonny would grab her, this could be anywhere anytime any day or night he would just come and grab her groom and spike. She was a fool for trusting him all these years. But it keeps coming, the memories get worse and worse as time goes on.

Chapter Two

Tabitha's mind kept racing back through the years, revisiting each moment that had led her to this point. As she cleared her throat she began to narrate her story onto a dictaphone to record her notes. After printing she picked up the envelope ready to file it, yet to decide what to do with it afterward. But for now it stays in her filing cabinet, she glances around her desk, her gaze landing on the younger photos of her and Jonny which she had found in a negative form due the photos had been stolen years before, but they forgot to take the slides. As she thought to herself __there must be no loose ends. After all this was now her legacy. The wide-eyed youthful images of their days out on the river boats and driving around in the car he had given her when he took her to Paris many times. But before she could finish dictating the adrenaline of reliving these moments was creating an inner anger within her, she had to keep a handle on herself and not give in to the temptation of acting upon her thoughts of fury and revenge. She had deep lacerations on her head and she could recall how each one was made, where and who. They were like notches to tick on her list of jobs that would be proclaimed one day. This was something that could change the very fabric of her life once she's told her story.

She soon begins to recall another more serious incident, "stop! don't say anything more!" as a figure enters the room as she's about to tell her story. She shrugs him off, the seconds ticking away like precious grains of sand, and begins anyway because she can't bottle it up any longer. This is going back decades; one sunny spring morning she was doing her usual school run early. She had to drive as it was a long way to walk with small children in tow, the pregnancy made her tired and parking was a nightmare. She would park down an estate and walk up a small hill to drop her children into school. The children were very young at this time, she was pregnant with her third child. Jonny had pestered her a lot around that year more than usual but she really wasn't paying much attention to him, due to memory loss most of the time as it happens, a woman came in once to her home when she had eight valentines cards signed J. She was accused of seeing him, which she denied. How could she know if he kept roofying her anyway, as far as she was concerned she had little recollection so her answers were honest. On this one particular morning Jonny and his driver were waiting by her parked car just moments after she dropped her child off, she had the toddler with her as she hadn't started preschool yet, the little girl was strapped into a pushchair and they headed back down the hill towards her car. Tabitha glanced around as she tried to avoid these two men who wanted to chat, Jonny jumped out of the car blocking her path and tried to sweet talk; gently presses his hand onto her wrist, he's trying to be pleasant but she was in a hurry, only he wouldn't take no for answer. She tried to narrow her focus and concentrate on the task at hand which was her day ahead, cutting through the panic that threatened to envelop her but she was soon put at ease with his charm. "You're going to be ok," he said. This was a period in her life she was suffering major memory loss so she didn't remember who he was, it didn't help he was made up with makeup to appear differently, which he often did in hindsight. Someone she had known her entire life, how could that be you wonder, that's a long story but it was a mix of two things, roofie and head trauma that had left her in a coma when younger, this story belied her tender years.

 She was trying to be polite but wanted to move on down the path to her car, as the big man was giving her uneasy vibes as well, he introduced himself as Shane, he had an odd accent that sounded like he was putting it on. Tabitha couldn't make out if it was put on as it didn't sound natural whatsoever. He really was creepy; her instincts and inner gut feelings knew something wasn't right. Her insides screamed he's dangerous but she couldn't remember so she was none the wiser. Jonny said "do you want to come for a drink she was like, no she tried to explain why;" no, i'm unable to right now and she was unable to recall why nevertheless she did get in the car unfortunately being persuaded further. With a trembling hand Jonny passed her a drink. She stated no at first it's too early, but reaching over she took it, it was a small orange juice carton, he mentioned "it's just one go on," She refused the beer then took the juice substitute. The mood he was in was upbeat. He became so persistent then he suddenly reached into a blue Range Rover grabbing an orange-juice in a small box with a straw. In the side door pocket she could see a man's clothes brush for some reason this stayed in her mind's eye. She recalled the car colour as she had mentioned it to him how unusual it was that seemed to panic Jonny as well. After a while she accepted the offer from his pressuring, "I need to go" she added, trying to explain she had things to do that day, but he wasn't taking no for an answer he was soon assisting her into the car with a shove. His face and hair looked odd but she brushed the thought aside. As they drove past the school the music was quite loud coming from the car and there were witnesses across the road being nosy at their gathering. Jonny had a sudden after thought and mentioned to Shane thus asserted "I told you not to get such a noticeable colour, oh well" he shrugged. He laughed but he wasn't being honest she could tell in his tone like he was hiding something. The more Tabitha looked at Jonny it looked like his long hair was in a ponytail to look shorter and something was odd about the tip of his nose. It looked different somehow and he definitely had make up on his

Object
face. She brushed it off as it was more common now for men to wear makeup. After a short period she succumbed to the drug that was laced in the orange juice, the big guy had lifted the baby and buggy up into the boot, a dangerous way to travel and suddenly she felt herself succumbing to the drug they slipped in her drink. As they drive past the infant school some of the parents see her in the back, the same way any nosy mothers do at a school run but this was her blessing but

she wasn't aware at this time the nosy mothers had told the police she was seen in this car. Unfortunately this was no good, perhaps Tabitha was unwilling to recall anything there could be no encounter to recall or furthermore even tell of subconsciously she had this memory blocked. She looked over at Jonny he was pulling a plastic bag up from under the seat, he then began to take items from it which through blurry eyes and realised he was putting on more makeup, he started with a five O'clock shadow using a dark shade to match his hair tone which was dark brown, once he finished getting that right he pinned his long hair up at the back so it now looked a short style, drew his brows on fatter and a different shape. By this point she said you look like a clown and laughed but he was taking it very seriously, he fixed the prosthetic tip of his nose into a different shape to his own, and then began to add these fake ear tips to his ears to which Tabitha found funny and said "SPOCK beam me up SPOCK!" while she was laughing at herself she was already forgetting where she was and that her child was even in the car. Everything was becoming less of a worry, the spike made her relax so much she was in and out of drowsiness. One of his fake ears kept falling off, the left one, he was like " I got to get this fucking ear to stay on is there any glue, and he licked it to create a suction sticking it back on top and held it for a while. She wondered if they were heading to the studios for a film as it wasn't unusual for him to get ready on the way for filming but he looked ridiculous. He wasn't convincing at all; he appeared like someone had taken a biro to a magazine and doodled facial hair all over it. Sometime later, perhaps an hour or more it wasn't long before they were in London, driving around town houses, Jonny seemed obsessed with popping in to see a woman he knew while in London, calls and messages he was making to find out what time she got home were happening. 'Tabitha thought why did she come out with these guys as she began to wake up from her dizzy slumber, feeling drunk yet she had not drunk anything but the orange juice, she may of had just one beer along the road but unclear at this point in memories, she mentioned she must indeed get back for the school run. It appeared his mood was calm but hostile about the call he had just had. He kept saying "she will be back soon," to his driver, "let's go back around to the road where she lives again." They already did one lap past the house to check the road and exit so they knew their escape route. " She will be there any minute" Jonny piped up. Hes closely watching a car parking up other side of the road, at that the driver pulls up and Jonny shouts "there she is, there she is, quick pass me that thingy in the front there," the driver passed something between the door using the seat and Johnny's jacket as a shield, Tabitha thought she seen a gun, yes she did see a gun but she was spinning about, it was a 39 calibre with a silencer on, he tried to hide it then braggingly showed her it and pointed it at the baby in the boot like a threat to keep her mouth shut, placing it in his trouser waistband but it was too big, so he unscrewed the suppressor, she was used to seeing guns, by now and knives, these things were part of the street, she didn't like people who felt the need to use

Mystery Man

weapons it felt very cowardly. It's not like the old wild west anymore, it's modern ridiculousness, it made her want to roll her eyes, thinking to herself he needs to grow up. She thought he was just showing off men can be real blagards in that realm of their lifestyle. She wasn't taking him seriously. Suddenly Jonny jumps out the back door to the right side of the 4x4 car onto the road. Across from the ladies house Tabitha sees Jonny running over the road into the gateway of a townhouse, it arrears that he's hitting her repeatedly his arms flying frantically, yes his arms were flying at her from all angles he fights like a girl she thought, at this the driver spots the struggle and reverses the car way back down the road to park up on the left two hundred yards perhaps, he didn't want Tabitha to witness it, then Shane sits and waits engine still running. He keeps checking the rear view mirror at Tabitha, checking she isn't able to witness anything that said her state of being roofied did that anyway and he had great faith in the drugs they used. The sun was out oddly for that time of year, so Tabitha was leaning back comfortably in the back seat feeling incredibly relaxed. She was chatting to the driver, he was looking intensely forward at what Jonny was up to, he wasn't focussing on Tabitha's chatter much but he still kept looking in the rear view mirror at her, while he was keeping his eye out in the face of turmoil, he was nervous about what Jonny was up to. The air crackled with his anticipation. Suddenly there was a loud bang she's not sure if it happened once or twice but it was loud. Shane looked white with shock he glanced in the mirror at her once more, then turned around and said you better keep your fucking mouth shut now or you'll be next. She had no idea what he was on about, all of sudden he was concerned for her safety, no more likely his own. She laughed and said in response, did you hear that car backfire, omg? Shane suddenly improvised and said yes old banger and smiled, but he was looking white faced and panicked by this time. Jonny hastily comes back to the car, hands over the gun and the driver slips it back under the seat into a cloth bag, as he does so he looks back at Tabitha and notices her watching closely his every move. Jonnys acting very calm, like he just grabbed some snacks or something so he was not shaken by the loud bang. The driver sparks up and says, "Did you hear that car backfire? She heard it.. Letting him know in an indirect way. She was not with it at all and made no head nor tail of the incident whatsoever anyway. But they had great faith in the fact the roofy would wipe her memory. Jonny says drive lets go, he pulls out fast and suddenly Jonny says with a calm voice no man just go steady normal speed, stop slow right down here she said she wont talk well she wont talk now fucking bitch. As they rubberneck past the house he points to a body in dark clothing laying on the pathway of the house, all she could see was a body in a fetal position laying on their side, feet toward the gate, head toward the door. She could see someone's bottom in dark trousers, she wasn't sure if it was a man or woman though. She didn't realise it was the same person Jonny was just hitting, this actual drug literally takes you from moment to moment and the past doesn't exist. The body had A long coat pulled up over their body like a blanket kinda messy-ly hung. He points and says angrily "see that fucking cunt, do you wanna be like that fucking cunt, do you? Well? " She looks out the window at the body and says "who is that, what do you mean?" Her innocent mind says that a homeless person dismissing the thought process and wondering if it is an appropriate spot to sleep there, forgetting the loud gunshot because she thought it was a car backfired. She was stupefied and unable to process anything by this point, ___ " it's someone's doorway she spouted" Jonny laughed reaching his arm over her shoulder, "no, don't worry" that embargo he placed upon her. "That won't happen to you" he reassured her, as he leaned over and kissed her on the cheek. Why was she dragged along to this horrendous ordeal anyway, why risk her being a witness, why bring her how can she be part of the cover up what was her role, what was the point was she there to

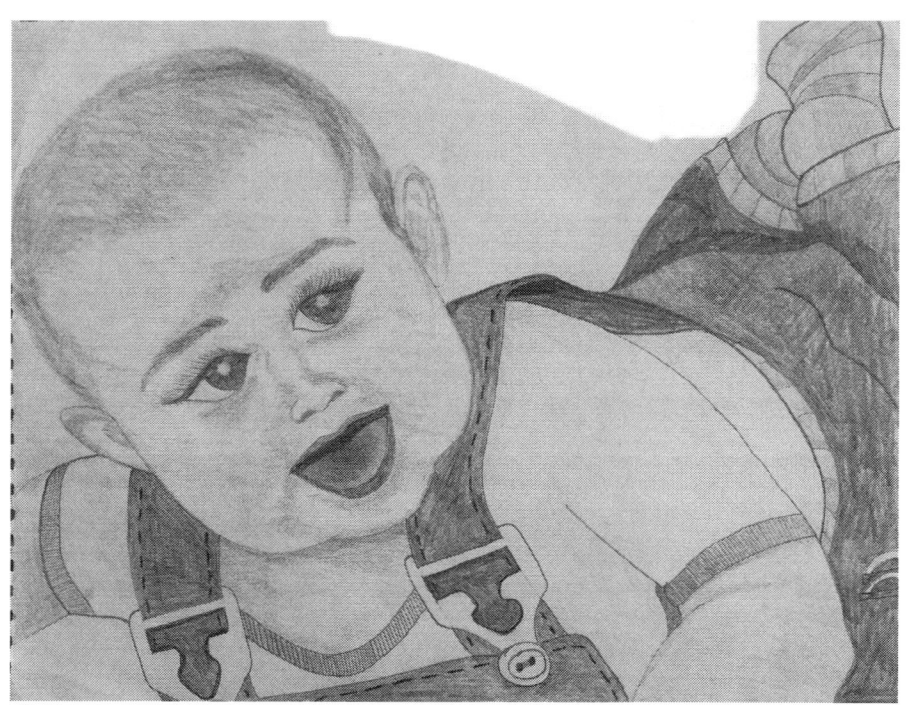

Baby On Board

make it look innocent , does he deeply desire to be helped from his mental state, what she didn't understand if he was crying for help to be stopped, well it seemed that way. The baby traveling in the back didn't wake up all day, that was also alarming but she couldn't do anything while feeling lightheaded. How dare they risk the baby girl in the back with a loaded gun in the car. Jonny kept saying to her, "your baby is there ok she's safe she's asleep" like suddenly he would be so merciful. Shame he was unwilling to show mercy on the lady he just shot point blank. But all those thoughts in that moment were suppressed. Her trying to rationalize what she saw was as impossible as making the police see the truth in front of them now. The human mind wants to only see the good in things. Just before they reach the end of the road and turn right, the driver suddenly says "I'm not gonna lie, I'm absolutely bricking it, shitting myself mate, what if the police pass us?" This was the first time she ever saw the bodyguard afraid it seems his biggest fear was the police.

_"Stop worrying man" Jonny piped up, "keep going, turn right here as they get to the end of the road they head out right," Tabitha replied to the driver, she wasn't sure of his name she'd only ever met him while being spiked well most of the time anyway, *but she find herself repeating the same questions each time they met asking him what is his name.* So with an innocent response she asked Shane "what are you worried about?" He paused for a second then improvised again replying with "I've no tax, mot, or insurance," as he gives Jonny a odd side eye look in the mirror, she knew how to act non suspicious. Tabitha spotted all these mistakes... but she was good at acting aloof, She replied; "don't worry about it, I've had cars without mot and tax in the past." __just because she forgot it had run out she was never been pulled over before so it's unlikely. She was so unaware that Jonny had just shot a woman dead on her doorstep in broad daylight, Tabitha was oblivious who where or why all this was happening. It took her three decades to remember it so even then she had started with no names to these faces she had in her memories, but it all came crashing at once, finally she twigged she was another journalist just like Jonny's side job, so that's how he knew her, but the real question was why?

They drive off into a secluded spot shes semi-conscious at this stage, shes laying back on the rear seat of the 4x4 and they had took her clothes off, as she opens her eyes and looked down she was half out the back door of the back seat, suddenly Jonny notices "shes pregnant" with a shocked voice, she was so slim her clothes covered the bump half way along her pregnancy but Shane piped up "I dont care" and raped her anyway, he placed her on her belly and Jonny told him to not do it that way it would hurt the baby, but why was he worried when rape is rape you aren't supposed to care, so Shane turns her over and once hes finished he glances right at Jonny to make sure he wasn't looking and gives her pregnant belly one hard punch. Afterward __ then it's Jonny's turn . After the two men raped her another car pulls up into the field behind them, then a third man approaches and speaks to Jonny, he was the man back and forth on the phone by the ladies house, Jonny had just called the man half an hour or so before to meet them there, to swap cars. In a haste Jonny orders the man who brought the second car-

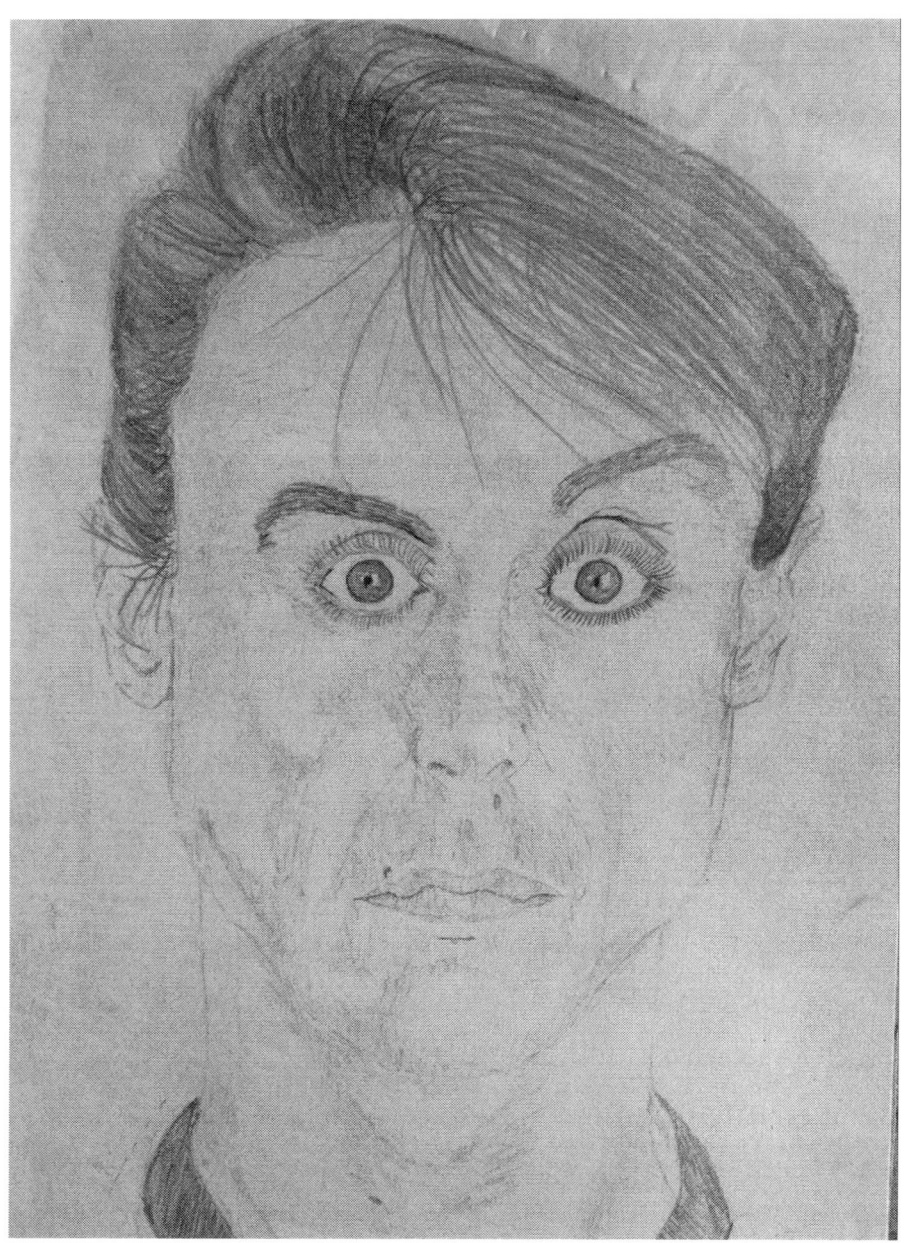

The Third Man
to burn and get rid of the blue Range Rover there and then, in that field, she can't recall if they waited around to drive him along too, maybe that's possible as she would have passed out again, or if he did

it elsewhere and they collected him after, the missing parts can come later or not at all if she was unconscious of course. Still it was carefully planned out, he knew the police weren't very good at investigations due to he'd got away with things before and by now he knew they just don't look for clues like you'd imagine in the crime series. In the dim light her eyes could just focus on what was happening to her, but she knew enough but wasn't aware she would not remember any of it tomorrow. Jonny's suit had seen better days, as he stood there staring at the car about to be destroyed, and entrusted to this third man. His words echo in her ears "burn it!" The weight of what he'd just done and involved them all in was much to bear, he took a deep breath and tossed his clothes into the car about to be destroyed with traces of blood on them. He must have felt a strange feeling of relief afterward knowing she could no longer talk. Even though the other two men looked very serious Jonny continued to laugh and joke like it was absolutely nothing to him. He must have felt a significant step forward as a new beginning. So they all walk back to the other vehicle and soon head back to the town Tabitha lives to drop her home.   Tabitha was unable to be sure if she had seen the third man before but he was familiar this did keep playing on her mind. His face is still a blur but each day a little clearer in her memories. Just moments before she was flopping around as Shane was redressing her, like a tangible force compelling her to speak, her life was spiraling into uncertainty, in that moment she blurted out to the third man "I know you!" at that she felt herself drifting back into a deep sleep, her eyes rolling back falling backward as Shane catches her. The third man had on a cap and short cropped hair, brown, he had a Romanian look but an English accent. As she did so she had caught a glimpse of Jonny as he was pulling off the tip of a prosthetic nose, and wiped away all the makeup letting his hair down long, he pulled off one prosthetic ear "shit i've lost one is it in the car?" Worrying, he left behind some clues. The hushed tones of Jonny's struggles with mental illness lay lurking, his eyes flickering like they were giving away his panic, along with his shaking hands. By this time the sun had gone away behind the clouds and it felt like drizzle but she wasn't too sure as the spike makes a victim lose feelings of senses. Jonny hadn't always been her abuser, but there was no empathy inside Jonny. What you see of tears is purely an act he's mastered. He once had a kinder side but he couldn't keep it up very long. Something would snap in his head plus you could see it in his eyes he'd blink when he was nervous of being caught out, like a minor flutter of his poker face breaking. They take the second car and go somewhere for a few hours but Tabitha hasn't remembered it all yet, she wakes up when they head back around the motorway to collect the third man, he hops in back seat opposite, and is introduced to Tabitha, Jonny's laughing with joy "yeah man we did it told you we could pull it off we'll get some coke to celebrate tomorrow," the third man replied i'm knackered i've walked for four hours. They head back to his town where she can't recall but she will, they drop him to a road and collect a third car they had dropped off the night before she had overheard Jonny asking Shane if he had done it he was like yea. Their plan went like clockwork. They all got out of the second car standing by the boot, it was open and the child was still asleep in the pushchair but Tabitha was too spiked herself to be aware anything was wrong. The third man mentioned to Jonny why bring a pregnant woman and child to this, "a decoy man." They discussed how the third man left his jacket at work and locked his door and exited via a different exit to go unnoticed and undisturbed so his alibi was that he was at work when in fact he was burning the getaway car. He seemed confident, Jonny replied she won't remember any of this, don't worry. He offered for him to have a go on her he declined "you look at fanny's all day ha Jonny laughed. Yea sumat like that. The third man was worried for the unborn child and that she was drugged it seemed. The conversation headed into a direction that he didn't care about the woman shot. He mentioned he hates her, Jonny quickly corrected him saying "you hated past tense man" laughing again, adding they will party the next day and have loads of coke to celebrate her death. She was getting the impression he was the boyfriend of the lady shot but it wasn't clear her head was spinning; she'd be unconscious again as soon as they were sat in the third car. She had a good look at his face and remembers it like she's looking at him today. How could someone's boyfriend do that to her and why, what was Jonny's anger towards her too? She had no idea of her or her childrens fate that day. But the drug was keeping away any concerns for her own well being. There was no fight or flight feeling it suppresses all that. The driver seemed like he was just there because he was up to his neck in it himself anyway so he also had something to lose, his freedom by the sounds of it. That was their biggest fear… …….PRISON! Of course they wouldn't like to be on the receiving end of all they put Tabitha through since being a child.

The only clue left behind was the prosthetic ear that kept falling off Jonny's ear. But his make up went down a treat and convinced the papers the CCTV was a real person, whoever the man was they were trying to set up anyway. That was another plan they were discussing how to set him up, drug him and take photos, plant the gun powder in his coat and so on. Jonny knew the police weren't into investigations like they show on TV so he knew he could tell them anything, they'd never suspect an actor let alone a billionaire. What's his motive? They dont have a clue about his rape club so why would they suspect him. The law leans heavily towards the wealthy, most of the time they will win most cases because money talks.

On the way home she must have passed out as her next memory was waking up in her bedroom. She recalled Jonny holding her baby girl on the landing and asking which room was hers as she pointed to the room he carried her to bed. She followed him in he said I'll fucking throw her in a minute if you dont hurry up, at that he violently threw the baby girl face down onto the bed she woke up momentarily and cried her neck hurt. Those evil men had her in that chair drugged all day and night. Tabitha wakes up in the early hours and goes to check on the children asleep, she felt sick with a banging head, the boy was in bed tucked in perfectly, he must have climbed in by himself as Jonny didn't get her home in time for school run. When she walks down the long landing entering the bedroom of the girl she is face down on top of the blankets shoes on and dead still, this alarmed her as she would always bath pj's and bedtime the children with a story book before sleep. She rushed to her, giving her a gentle shake to make sure ' breathing and she woke up, with a relief she settled her with a warm bottle of milk, probably the only thing since breakfast the poor child had no thanks to the monsters. As she took off her little shoes and dressed her in her pjs then tucked her under the warm blankets, she had always been asleep in the back of the car. Jonny kept saying "there's your baby look shes fine shes fine ok." As if to reassure her on the murderous road trip. The next morning she awoke blank to the day and night before, but this time she was very unwell, her belly is in pain from the thump, and she's concerned she may lose the baby so she rests a few days. She thought something was wrong with the baby and was concerned she had flu, but

unbeknown to her the last 24 hrs were again yet another trauma and she had lost a day, her body remembered but her memory was gone. The next morning her son said "mummy can you collect me from school? I was scared coming home alone and the boys next door had to lift me into the window to get in the house so I could go to bed."
 " What are you talking about? I always get you, I'd never leave you, are you sure it wasn't a bad dream?" She had no idea about the entire day before in fact she thought it was monday again. It was a miracle he got home safely, luckily playing with the older boys next door saved his life that day. There was a bowl on the kitchen table of milk and cereal. He had made himself tea when home alone the night before but Tabitha had just thought he got up early and made breakfast. It was a confusing time she thought perhaps she had the flu and that was why she felt so unwell. How can a roofie wipe away days at a time, so much lost time, she was starting to just think she had a scatty baby brain with a cross of stress. Somehow she always had this one memory that never went away of seeing Jonny hitting a woman in her doorway fists flying everywhere, he was raging and that image stuck with her but she had never connected it with the death of the lady on the news. She hardly ever watched the news so things like would skim over her head, the TV maybe on in the background but she didn't ever pay attention enough to get into it. It wasn't the first time she saw him beating up women out of nights out; this was to do with drug dealing she was guessing and didn't think anything of it that comes with the territory.

 The trafficking had started when she was schoolgirl, this carried on till her early forties there was no set rule when they wanted her they would take her from any situation, she could be taken from dinner out with friends, a bar a club, or a afternoon walk they would come get her, drug her and she's not recall anything, the only memory is the brutal cuts and bruises which are permanent scars, fag burns and stab wounds, along with lots of head splitting scars that she couldn't account for. The odd sickness she thought was flu was her healing from abuse. Jonny had started the abuse when she was a child, just when she felt like she had recalled it all she would remember more details and realised it began a lot younger than she first thought, from Jonny bringing her panda pops drugged them, she was getting painful water infections and stinging from the rapes but she didnt recall begin raped so it made no sense. Even on school trips she would see him, everywhere she went over the years he would appear, this was no coincidence how he can turn up to road trips and holidays abroad he was always there, clubs, pubs, and even family gatherings he wormed his way into her life. The drs examined her when was a girl and said she must have done it on the cross bar of her bike. One moring while waiting for the bus he came to the back seat with her and just before running off before it left he said, "i'm going to rape your mum today she wont remember as i've drugged her. " Tabitaha told the bus driver what he said and she promised to report it but nothing came of it. He was sick from the start but she only remembered the nice times due to he roofied her so much while performing the evil acts she couldn't recall any of that. One of the memories almost resurfaced as she digressed her story back. As the years had passed she was reading up on this crime due to the memories in the online headlines, she felt connected somehow, she discovered that a man had pretended to be the driver of the fiat, the night in the tunnel and had turned out he drove out to a secluded spot and set himself on fire. This felt unrealistic the only way anyone could do that is to be roofied unconscious to not feel it and not struggle it screamed: made to look like a suicide anyway, and she knew at this point he wasnt even there who are all these false stories false drivers coming forward saying they drove the car, why that made zero sense why on earth would anyone want to get mixed up in that drama no way not if responsible unless they were paid large sums of cash and the only person who would benefit from this is Jonny and his mate. Also the only person rich enough, as money will buy freedom. There were by this time some awful stories in the paper about the father of Odie, she couldn't see them two men at all even though she sees that side in Jonny and his mates until someone does it to her or she sees it she only believes what she experiences herself. Tabitha had seen Hamad was a heartbroken father who lost his son crying tears of pain so she never saw the other side people talk about, all she knows is that Jonny has contacts in the papers and anything he wants printed he can pay and it's done. Anything ! There is always a way to print lies when you have the money to cover the fact they may get sued. So these horrific memories of witnessing violent deaths and murders that have smothered the papers for months at a time are suddenly creeping into her mind. She finally got to the stage where she had to report the doctor as he was playing dirty with his power, telling her if she didn't stop speaking about all this he could section her, knowing full well he's up to his neck deep in this sordid sex trafficking rig now he is only trying to save his own back. He knew about the kids being harmed so why was he covering for them still? A full investigation may happen if he doesn't back off and leave her alone. Tabitha had to tell authorities about him, she was sick of laying down and being walked over by these men, the thing is Jonny may go after him for helping her. After all Jonny owns these women under him, mess with the system and the same thing will happen to the Doctor as it did to the woman on her doorstep. Tabitha is at the point now she has to fight this alone, all he's done is hinder her and her children recovering from trauma by refusing to let her have a diagnosis she felt was ptsd, she couldn't go forward without that because then he knows very well she can then tell a counsellor all about what he's done and he needs to stop that therapy . He took her into his treatment room and threatened to section her, "I have the paperwork right here" he laughed off the statement "but I won't. if I wanted to I could" No more holding back his dirty secrets of his sexual fetishes in the treatment room. Why should she protect him any longer? Not meaning he was violent but violating her in a perverted way and watching her take a beating from these two men and protecting them by covering up what they did to her. The Doctor was one of Jonny's customers, when Jonny drugs, trafficking these women there are no limits to their ages, she knew this because it all started with Jonny herself when she was eight, eleven, and fifteen, and every year after that up until her early forties. He would call upon her, it wasn't always abuse.

There was a time he was deeply fond of her and kind in her teens and twenties but he couldn't keep up with his nice guy act for very long. He gave her many sentimental things. This was his way of hiding what he was really up to but needed to outwardly express it, he liked hiding in plain sight. But his secrets were seeping through the cracks. While the years passed as extra dreadful memories emerged she soon realised the good memories were becoming fewer and the reality of who Jonny really was revealed as his mask of kindness had finally fallen away. How did he become such a Hyde version of Jekyll ?

The company he kept were more like neanderthals, not much brain more braun but fat lardy braun and unattractive men, he surrounded himself with vile ugly men a lot, perhaps that was a mirror to who he

really was on the inside. But they didn't have much loyalty to him; they only had eyes for money, fame, and pervertedness; they were all damaged by mummy or daddy issues as what they had in common with one another. The real worriers are the ones who crawl from that childhood and do better in life than those who raised them. If you want to crawl from hell, do better, do good and good things will come, keep on that path of destruction and feel the wrath of what life throws back at you. They gave an insane man billions of pounds and watched him turn into an even bigger monster, what would have become of him if acting hadn't come along, he'd been a drug addict rapist the same as his men he surrounds himself with and highly likely of been shot on his doorstep like he did an innocent woman in her prime, a woman who seen him for who he truly was. The fact he has zero remorse about murdering and beating her is a big red flag that the world is in denial about and it's time they all woke up. This was a period where Tabitha had met almost every man in Hollywood including some Royals, yet she had figured it all out who was good and who was bad. The Royals ok they were raised with manners but she had seen for herself that they were a good family on the receiving end of the medias lies, and she'd figured out that the media was up to its neck, not all but a minority deeply dwelling within the rape club that Jonny kept close to him, look who posts the most kind things about Jonny and you'll find your sources. Those who write awful things about him most likely have good instincts and are aware of the stories but too afraid to pursue it. They will of course eventually keep tip offs on the shelf for a rainy day when more evidence comes to the surface so don't think they ignore stories sometimes it isn't the right time to tell. But this too will pass and this too will come to the surface for the world to see and finally see the real side of the man who
turned evil. As the mind unravels the truth over time it becomes more and more clear how much trauma was blocked but now unveiling it is a wonderful feeling, this must be bottled and kept for future reference, as Tabitha stops her recording for a moment to gather her next memory. Suddenly she blurts out loud, "I copped off two Princes! How on earth did I end up with two, not one , TWO Princes in my lifetime?"… O..m..g, gathering her thoughts in sheer shock as she recalls details. Every memory seems to shock her more each time, you'd think she would be used to them by now, some were mundane, while others made her grimace. One of which she was forced by

Jonny and his bodyguard, not the Princes fault he was as misled as she, he may not have known she was roofied into submission. This made sense now what their father meant by "my sons" She had asked him how he knew her name. He reminded her "my sons," covering his mouth from others listening and laughed as she reached out and held his hand among the crowd in London, while she stood behind the rope that separated them. She was glad he found it funny, she couldn't tell if it was reality or a dream during the moment, that's what a roofie is like it feels like you're dreaming. He must have been spiked otherwise why on earth and how on earth did they convince him to run into a field and jump in like the water was cold. That day Jonny had taken her there, as he waited to walk her out of the crowd afterward, trying to hide himself from being spotted by the public while he was with her. What she does recall was set up by Jonny, he sent his bodyguard to distract the prince's bodyguard. He was being really loud in the bar drawing all attention onto him while Jonny walked Tabitha out back, then sent the prince to her, he was filming it, he was trying to set up the prince to look bad, Jonny was committing treason and used Tabitha as his weakness to seduce the prince. She wasn't interested in sex, but he came to her, grabbed her and spun her over onto him hastily, so she got it over with as quickly as possible, no romance. It felt robotic and with Jonny holding the camera standing back, she just thought what an asshole to do this to this man, if she didn't she'd be beaten bloody again. The prince seemed to want to talk during it which was odd making conversation at a moment like this, she gave him the look… of shut the fk up. When they got back to the bar Shane began to shout his mouth to the entire pub he lost his virginity laughing, he made a public mockery of him. The drug took away all feelings anyway. So she smacked his bum afterward and that set him off trotting back to the pub, thinking she did it a little hard as his feet left the ground, he giggled and ran back to the pub. It was another case of abuse from Jonny and his bodyguard, she can't blame the prince for this one he was as much an innocent victim as she was, the only advantage she had was the roofy they spiked her with, it took away her feelings, and incidentally her memory. It's easy to deal with the men who forced her and added violence she can oddly enough deal with that, the men she feels she may have hurt, this brings her sadness. But in hindsight he was laughing about it and patted on the back with a big grin on his face, so hopefully it didn't scar him. Jonny had ruined her life. But she wasn't leaving this world without telling her life story, she may as well put the record straight and do her best to fix what these horrible men did to her and many others. History may as well be written correctly after all the propaganda. She's pretty sure Jonny's bodyguard roofied the Prince and coerced him into it.

All memories were flooding in all at once and everything around her was triggering them. Jonny would show her photos of Odie on his phone and tried to tell her about that day but nothing would come to surface back then. However, the amnesia was drifting away. Not only the skull fracture was healed but her brain was reconnecting to its past memories as the metaphorical fog drifted away. Her mind was filling in the missing pieces, remembering back to the night in the champagne bath with Jonny in his suit and her naked rolling around while the photos were shot. She recalled being all sticky, the parts she first recalled where those intimate details were still missing, finally it resurfaced clear as if it happened last night. This one came back in huge gaps years apart in fact. At first she was uncomfortable but then the roofy kicked in as her inhibitions quickly settled. There was once a side to him that had been gentle, suddenly thus a side that was evil. Was he even aware of the two personalities he had. Suppose she will never fully know. His grandparents were always kind to Tabitha growing up, the nicer ones were Jonny's fathers side who ran the shop, the other grandfather was very quiet but you'd hear him shout at Jonny's brother a bit. The older generations knew better but something was amiss with him since childhood. It appeared he kept one side of grandparents secret his mothers side never got publicly recognised and false names given to the media, but she was starting to understand that's what they do with celebrities, change their past and hide who they really were, it was to protect them. Incidentally it was such a pity he couldn't have just been the kind version of himself all the time. That version of himself would have been worth saving, consequently the evil side was beyond help, while she grappled with the thoughts was it even possible for him to ever have any feelings whatsoever, especially since things seemed rather hopeless. One thing she had noticed was that from her young teens to this day it was the same blond haired photographer, was around the same age as Jonny , who was always hanging out drinking with Jonny the same man who did the photo shoots as well as the fake news posting he was in France when sometimes it was England the event happened at. He must be the only one Jonny trusts perhaps hes fully aware of the rape club as well or even part of it to be so trusted on these drink and drugs benders Jonnys is always on. Some of Jonny's friends who he fell out with would also end up in sticky situations and end up in the news under a terrible headline. It was beginning to look like he was setting people up to look bad, spike them, send them into situations of shoplifting or adultery, take photos and suddenly they made the front page. It was no coincidence how his articles for the papers always hit the front page; he wasn't just lucky he was creating the news. Some of the news articles online Tabitha was with Jonny while he captured those photos so by time she saw it she knew it was him writing articles. His connections in the local papers were an ideal way for him to express his spitefulness abusing his position of authority. Furthermore he was now a danger to himself; it was only a matter of time before Mi5 and Mi6 were onto him. She was angry but she refused to act on it, she can't bring herself to hurt him, because she's not the same as him, thoughts may flash in anger but deep down she won't allow herself to have that on her conscience. Better to walk away and let them dig their own hole. What will happen? It's inevitable some fathers of these girls who have been victim to him will find him one day, and deal with it underground, will his death be as famous as the victims he killed? No doubt, but it will probably be covered up regardless. Even seeing him killed would be sad because there was once a nice person behind the evil he evolved into. *He ruined himself and took everyone around him with him.*

Chapter Three

With the public help platform Tabitha had made, she was able to help and give advice to other victims who had suffered and guide them not to become the same way Jonny and his friends had gone down the dark path. This platform was rather valuable as it had given her a list of names and addresses and a list of their crimes committed. The police had proven they were no longer beneficial to sexual violence they were only interested in fraud. Even murder was not important to the law which was apparent common knowledge of the villains which is how they keep getting away with it. They know the police restrict the investigation fully or funding means they are unable to. While Jonny was in the spotlight most of his life his crimes were lurking in the shadows waiting to be discovered. Enemies within the same towns who lurked in the doorways of clubs watching his every move. Most killers were difficult to catch due to there being no personal connections between the killers and the victims but in this matter this was not the case his victims were well known and close to him. His professional goals didn't outweigh his sexual desires therefore he risked it all many times giving total faith in the drugs that made the victims forget. Accolades to him were important but his honor of being a gangster was higher. The feeling of control was in the criminal world where the acting roles left him under direction, that being said to a narcissist isn't fully in control and this unsettles them. His natural antagonism over ruled his personal life and personality he'd lost control of himself and was only getting worse with age, but one things for sure she knew the faces on the tv were the same men in the rape club. She had now identified them. She had evolved to a new way of thinking and retribution was on their horizon.

*Tabitha's compelling memories became unambiguous*____ This case drew national attention to such cases about how the justice system had to give itself a shake up including work better at improving their investigation of trafficking crimes in the uk. His life was subject to documentaries and films alike that pasted a fake image of who he really was, down to the fraudulent hushing of women victims in his reign.

Tabitha finally talks about strength and its true purpose. Men are often admired for their physical strength, their capacity to push limits, and their ability to shoulder heavy burdens. This strength is a gift, one that can be a force for the good in the world. Men possess an undeniable physical power. They have the ability to protect, to build, to lead. But true strength is not measured by how much force one can exert on others; it is measured by how much power of a man lies in his ability to be protective and supportive, not in overpowering those who are physically weaker. There is a disturbing paradox in society where some men instead of using their strength to uplift they use it to dominate.

Tabitha was still processing the long term abuse; women do not get better with help but get better by helping themselves. The system right now leans heavily towards helping the abusers not the victims, but this law will hopefully one day be overruled. The justice system is broken and needs to be shaken up. Raise your children with love not hate so they become better adults when they step out alone into the world remember; love creates kind wonderful human beings, hate and cruelty can create monsters.

Any man can make a mistake and acknowledging that mistake can lead to forgiveness over time. However , continuing to repeat the same errors is a form of insanity. Ultimately, it seems that some men lack the ability to feel empathy for anyone but themselves. This instability to empathise not only harms their relationships but also stunts personal growth.. It creates a cycle of misunderstanding and conflict, resulting in a society where kindness and compassion are overshadowed by self-interest. Cultivating empathy is essential, as it allows us to connect with others on a deeper level and fosters a sense of community. By embracing our shared humanity, we can break free from this pattern and build a more understanding and caring world. Using your power to help instead of hindering will not only be a better way of feeding your self love, even if you cannot help the way you are you can rewire the way you act to achieve the same self love, but to be kind to others; then they'll love you too or at least be kind. Again it represents a profound misuse of the strength granted to humanity, transforming a gift into a weapon. Use your strength for the greater good, ensuring that our legacy is one of love.

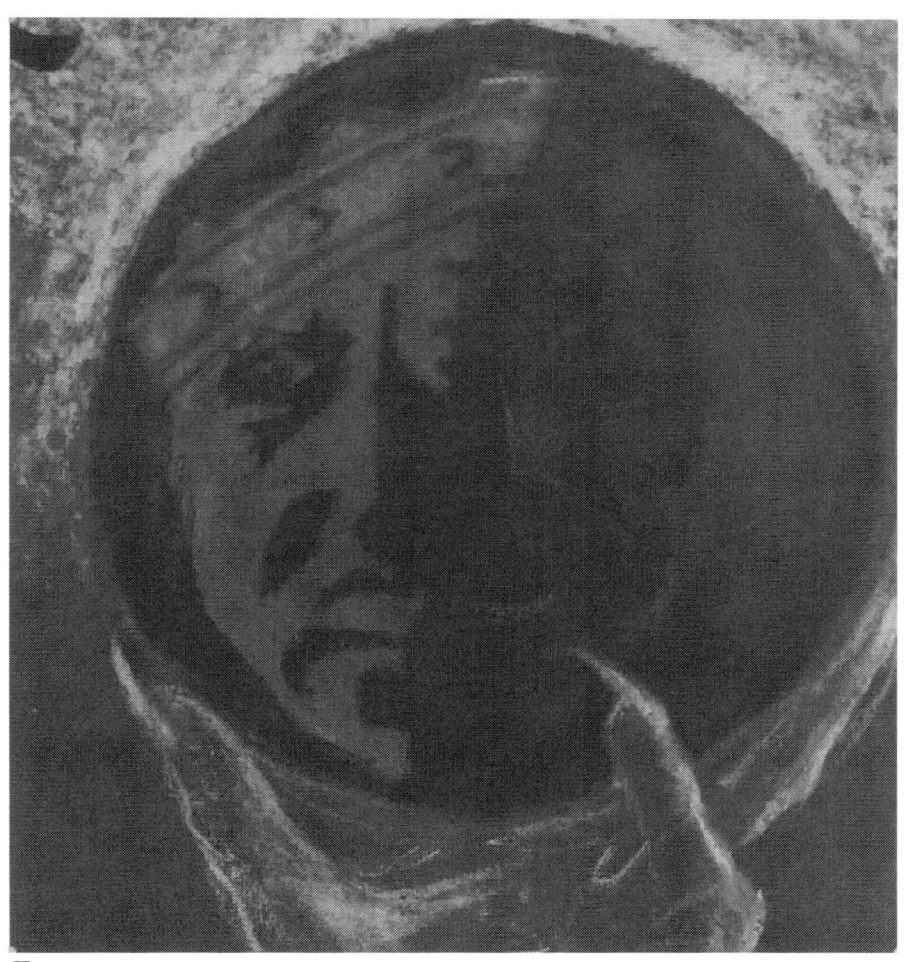

Foresee

River Farm
Jonny's name had carried an unsettling weight in the village growing up where Tabitha lived, regularly he'd come to visit his grandparents on both sides who lived there. From a young age he would often stay there visiting them long term. The hushed tones how people spoke about his mental illness and her cousins had warned her about, that he

had and to avoid him, he was trouble they told her they urged her to stay away. She had asked her cousin if he was a predator and her reply was "I think so." Their voices thick with concern. Tabitha with an innocence of youth resolved to heed their warnings, yet fate had a different plan. Despite her efforts to keep her distance, Jonny remained an unwilling specter in her life. He pursued her relentlessly, his presence weaving into her world like the uninvited chill of winter. He was charming and this was hard to resist sometimes, but soon found herself entwined in a complicated fate that would change her life forever. Before long she anticipated danger that sent her life spiralling out of control. In the face of turmoil Johnny's mother stepped in a few times to stop them but it was unavoidable in the very end. Tabitha's decisions echoed through the corridors of her entire life. She carried the burden of her secret shielding it from prying eyes of the world around her and never spoke a word to a soul. So she guarded the truth and did her best to carry on with a normal life as possible. Today the air could be cracked with anticipation, a harbinger of revelations yet to come. The secret rested heavily on her heart, intertwined with her very being, waiting for the moment it could no longer be confined to the shadows of her memory.

Chapter four

Tabitha sat in her mothers living room, the ticking of the clocks echoed like a heartbeat, a reminder of her past where that was the sound she grew up with many clocks on the wall, even when Jonny was there when they hung out when she was a teenager that was the sound and the quietness of the village they lived. Then there would be the loud chimes of the village hall clock next door that made them both jump, then fits of laughter because they knew they should be used to it by now but it always made them jump. They would be so bored sometimes they would just eye through the glass vase by flickering candlelight listening to the mix tapes he used to make for her. The memories, the love, the pain and the secrets. She glanced around the room, her glaze landing on an old photo of him and the resentment in her eyes felt ghostly. Just as she thought the evening was calm a suddenly a figure burst through the gate as she heard its clatter, there was a knock at the door. She approached and opened it wearily and stood there was a figure of a man, older now but unmistakingly it was Jonny. A fierce determination in his gaze. You have to know the truth he proclaimed, his voice strong yet trembling. Tabitha froze, her heart pounding, her secret tethering on the edge of revelation. The room erupted in murmurs, shock etched on everyone of her children's faces desperate for acknowledgment of what lay between them. With the weight of the past plunging them into darkness and confusion. In that proverbial moment, the secrets, the lies, and the truths hung suspended in the doorway, leaving everyone hanging. His presents descended like a thick fog. In that pivotal moment would Jonny reveal what needed to be said, or was it already too late? Tabitha froze, her heart pounding with the weight of the past pressing down on her she was holding her breath, then in the suspense, Tabitha finally whispered, "Jonny, I__" but hes furious as she realises she had to quickly get a word in before he went off on a rant at her, "you made Odie rape me in the apartment that day!" with a fury in her tone and a deep murderous look in her eyes. His eyes widened with surprise that she remembers it all, "YOU FUCKING BITCH!" knowing his game was up, she calmly turns to face him and says "Jonny, _____I think the word you're looking for is touché."

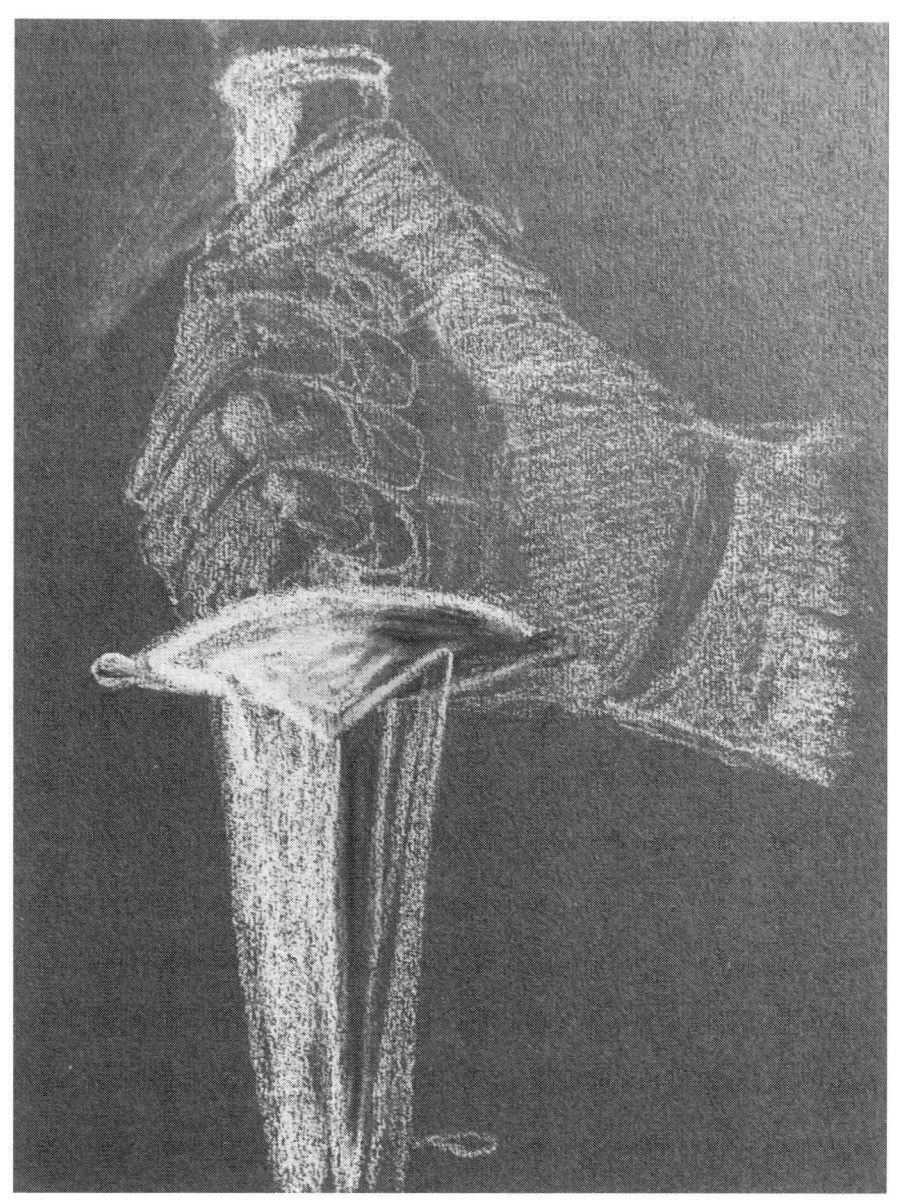

The Betrayal
Midway Epilogue
There are varying forms of human trafficking, slavery and sexual misconduct. There is a hidden count of victims due to its secrecy so therefore it's hard to report on and the system often doesn't listen or provide ample help for victims a lot of the time. The severe forms of

trafficking involving children and women, when the vicitim is unconcious remember 'nobody pays for rape' or asks for it for that matter. The victims don't get paid, they don't even remember it happened, the only signs are injuries and DNA left behind. A lot of these men get caught due to their films along with taking photos so they have the proof which can help a case, some of them collect trophies, jewelry or locks of hair from victims. A lot of men will brag about it too therefore they get caught that way. There is always a loose end to their circle of trust. Those loose tongued men are the ones unknowingly who help catch these groups. This can happen as a form of coercion where sometimes the victims form a bond with the predator who exploits vulnerability; they use the victims as a combatant to pass through as a normal looking family when being trafficked abroad under the guise as a family. The drugs they force into them keep the victims calm and are not always unconscious. So not only do they forget it all but it's a coping mechanism for what they dont know doesnt hurt them, and this benefits the criminals which is the main goal in not being caught. The government opposes such crimes but the demand for commercial sex still exists. Each year more than two million children are sexually exploited in the global sex trade. The crimes often slip through the cracks of weak law enforcement. This dehumanising has a knock on effect on the victims, furthermore modern day slavery must be stopped. Traffickers do not discriminate sex , gender or age; this could happen to anyone and it can come under the form of an ordinary job from the outside. It will mostly be involuntarily via intimidation and threats. Or simply an offer of an innocent drink from a stranger or somebody you know at the bar, this can also be disguised under the label domestic servitude.

 This book was written to help bring awareness to how crime goes undetected and how easy it is for criminals to slip through the prying eyes of the law. Using a high profile antagonist to show how easy that can be for anyone not just the guy who lives down the road but someone who may have trust in and no idea what's really going on behind closed doors. They get themselves involved deep into your life with vanity, lies and manipulation. It was Tabitha's diary that she never missed a day of jotting into that first rang alarm bells that she was missing days and nights. She began to jot things down as messages to herself before sleep and in the mornings even with a black out she had the proof, she had noted the abuse that went down the night before knowing she would not recall it. This being how she finally discovered the truth. Detectives grappled with the cases all those years, consequently couldn't solve them.

Fictional names and places that sound familiar to real life are merely bogus. Created to give an insight of how cases are often overlooked and the reasons being were often cover ups, lies from those involved and corruption within the law. Due to how unruly those in power use and abuse the system for their own benefits. This includes treason and perjury. This book is to bring awareness to how the underworld works right under your nose within a hidden environment. Victims of abuse must never feel unheard by the system, being told to just let it go is not a solution. Keep your aspirations high, unlike the character who was unaware of his self inflated estimate of his own knowledge which made him believe he was more powerful than the law when in fact it was equitable as copious amounts of cash being handed out as hush money to high profile men written into the books under charity. When analysing the situation, who is to blame, was it the drunk driver who lost control or was it a knock on effect of the celebrity ordering to knock off the press from their bike, who then hit the other car; that upset the driver into a high speed frenzy. You decide, or just the drink and an accident, you the people are the jury now . Thanks to CCTV and press photos inspiring stories for conspiracy theorists to explore that collaborated images of the Princess including images inside the tunnel that night. Allegedly, Including photos of a celebrity. Those photos were made public and thanks again to the press we could create this dramatised version of events to show how photos can tell a story just like how the press 'allegedly' print facts that aren't always correct. People with personality nuances can be hard to catch, as these traffickers can go hidden in plain sight, because high profile figures go unsuspected by the law.

The moral of the story in the very end; Tabitha took over five years to recall all the events in her life from the events where she was roofied. In the beginning she thought this must be it going back as far as childhood but in fact it was all coming back in a jumbled order. She came to realise she had been much younger when it all began with Jonny, therefore as each new memory came to the surface she had to slide things along and slot a new file in perhaps a few years earlier, but eventually it began to make sense until there was only a few pieces left of the puzzle to call life. She still didn't understand why he keeps following her; perhaps that's something she will never know and that's perfectly fine.

Tabitha now stood at the edge of a new beginning casting her gaze over the horizon, whispering secrets of freedom and renewal. The worry of the past had ebbed away, leaving behind only a soft imprint of what once was. With each passing day, she had unraveled the threads of old memories that had woven themselves tightly around her heart. The pain, the regret, the shadows of missed opportunities-they no longer embrace the lessons of yesterday. Her eyes reflected a fierce determination and unyielding hope. She faces the future with open arms . The past ahead was uncertain, yet it sparkled with possibilities that beckoned her to step forward. With a final deep breath now ready to write a new story filled with adventures, love, and the promise of a brighter tomorrow. She recalled these men all had odd fetishes, each one their own oddly sculpted idea of sexual fantasy. The Dr liked to play Doctor and take it all the way in control. Odie liked to be in control and call all the odds. The MP had a pregnancy risk taking fetish, so did Jonny he wanted to impregnate every female possible and that would be anyone with any looks, the only thing they had to have was a womb to incubate. His bodyguard was a full blown predator with a violence fetish. The other bodyguards tended to be similar; a violent job meant violent fetish. They came hand in glove, their jobs and sex lives intertwined. But over all they were living out fetishes in secret, for their wives and ordinary lives were hidden by this mask of deceit. The men Jonny used to take empowerment over Tabitha were in positions of taking control if she spoke out, therefore her doctor made sure she couldn't tell anyone, he put pay to her speaking to the police. He listened to her explaining from the start how she was remembering it all at that time she was unaware he was one of the memories yet to come, but he didn't try to hide it in fact he tried to tell her a couple times. Maybe he felt a little guilty; he was one of these men who had caused the long term trauma. She managed a coping mechanism by trying to think of the positive sides, there weren't many, but the non violent men she held no anger toward. She feels like she is owed more than an apology, without one she may be drawn towards some form of a wrath. She also knew which police members Jonny had lured into his boudoir of sexual fantasies they too were up to their necks in this big cover up. The secret society was immensely vast as it touched all corners of high profile jobs, it took Tabitha years to work out who was in Biggies club and who wasn't.

Five years later,...... Tabitha found herself at a bar waiting for her friends to arrive for a meet-and-greet, as she stood there, a familiar stranger approached, leaned in close and whispered, "You owe my friend money, now that debt belongs to me," "yes it does." agrees a tall stranger, their faces older, time had added weight to his features, grey thinner hair, he was the same man trying to make the same play. He was attempting to lure her into his car where they left off all those years ago. Knowing he had a pocket full of drugs, she turns to him, smiles "I've been waiting for this moment for a long time." she gives her bodyguard a nod, who had been watching the entire exchange. He discreetly reached down for his radio, calling in backup as the noise in the bar grew louder while music and chatter filled the air. While the racket of the boys in blue fly in from both front and rear doors, glass and bar stools start swinging, a brawl that Tabitha walks out of calmly, without a glance back. A small smile played on her lips as reached into her handbag, retrieving her favorite chocolate. She took a bite enjoying the moment the nut on the top with a sense of satisfaction, knowing they'll be locked up for a long time had an amusement about it.

She awakes early for work, the sunlight spilling in through the gap in her curtains, shielding her eyes with her hand, gradually opening them taking in her surroundings, the room was a vision of glamour, heavy velvet four-poster bed, and thick plush piled rugs laid on marble floors, arched doorways, and luxurious decor sparkled while the sunlight danced across them, this was her life now, a picture perfect cottage in France. She sits up in bed, turns to her husband and says, darling, I had the weirdest dream, it was about my life.

He turns over, pulling her into his arms, "hmmm, you can tell me all about it over breakfast," he replied with a warm smile. Feeling a sudden Deja-vu wash over her, in that moment she knew she was exactly where she was meant to be, a beautiful tapestry woven from dreams and reality, each thread carrying the promise of adventures yet to come.

The Mansion

Being trafficked around the world since you were age 11 has a profound effect on ones personality, it makes you hard, for that reason she may seem unloving at times but it's just you haven't seen much love so to survive, she had to dig deeper and recall her childhood home which was full of love and kindness and that's where you pull the strength from. Always fall back and do the right thing no matter how hard life is by doing so it's not about her it's about them.

    Tabitha decided to stand up and be a voice for the victims of all abuse, especially the children who are unable to understand or speak up for themselves. It's time someone did, additionally it's time the law listened and stopped shoving this kind of carry on under the rug, for what shame ? They should be ashamed for standing in the way of justice if you wont help them and just turn a blind eye to it all then that makes it look like they have a guilty conscience or a coward. Those kids cant help themselves or remember it due to the roofies the vile men use on them, this isnt just rape this torture and murders. It's time the law did something firm about these men, make an example of them and have them put to sleep like a dog. No human being should be allowed to live if they harm kids end of. It's not like a road accident after that's an entirely different kettle of fish, this is planned and executed down to the baby sitters who drug and harm the kids while they traffick the mother away.

    Let's begin; one of Jonny's drivers was dropping her off at home from a function. He walked into her house, which wasn't unusual and handed Tabitha a drink. This was evening early on, he then turned to her "I've slipped something into your drink so you won't remember what they do," before she could react to the burly man and Jonny barged in and violently dragged her out into the car. 30 min later she's at a local airbase she recognises due to always dropping Jonny there in her youth, she even knew where he kept his helicopter, all the pilots were in on this human trafficking and equally as vile mannered. She was forced into the hangar then into the plane. She must have fallen asleep on the way there as the next thing she remembers is shes being walked from the plane to a cargo container and locked inside by the burly man Jonny's chum. A woman who was American met us and came in with us.

The container was empty apart from rugs on the floor which indicated it being a frequently done thing. She took the victims phone numbers and pretended to be friendly to gain trust but the reason they do this is to call and make sure once you are returned home you don't recall anything from that party at the mansion. There was a lady sitting on her knees and a small child around five with her, she looked up mentioned " she usually isn't this still or quiet" as she looked at her daughter the little girls head flopped down semiconscious still sat cross legged on the floor next to her mother and in that moment her mothers head also dropped down out like a light. There was one more woman unsure if she was a victim or part of it but she was standing up, doesn't mean she wasn't part of it. But they bring just enough girls for just enough of their sick game.

    It wasn't long before they brang a car around and they were told to be silent and not speak to anyone. Heading out the gates of the airport a man questioned, Tabitha tried to speak up but she was told to shut up hastily by all in the car who were not victims. Tabitha must have passed out again and highly likely the others too. It wasn't long before they pulled up at the mansion, she couldn't see the woman or the little girl in the car, only herself Jonny and burly man 'the driver 'Jonny's mate. There must have been another car that took them probably to stop Tabitha talking to her as she would have gotten a name and pursued her and Jonny knew this therefore he took extra precautions to get this done right. As they come up toward the mansion they stop at the bottom of the track, the drive that leads up to the big house seemed worn and long. It was pretty but upon inspection as they drove closer Jonny said look we're going in there to a party and makes it sound like he's taking her there for fun but he flips from nice to psycho all the time so that Mr nice guy doesn't stay around long. They park up and walk towards the house up the wide steps and up some more to the enormous front door where a colored man comes out and grabs Tabitha; arms around her tight squeeze and says in her face "are you ready for a freaking crazy time?" he seemed like he was on drugs and wired. She couldn't tell if he was mad or manic. Jonny corrected him and said take it steady man you don't want to frighten her off just yet. As they entered the foyer there were these big stairs, two sets winding from both sides up to a landing that looked down over a chandelier but it was all in poor repair. The place looked tired and its once glam elegance was starting to fade which was sad. It was a castle that was now cursed, the insides matching the violence of what horrors were to come, upon entering a home without a blessing from a Irish girl who had this bless this house and all who live in it, didn't happen that day. She didn't feel it and didn't do it. But it's an old tradition her family always goes to new homes. And it works, it really works and makes a home lucky.

They walk along through some corridors and a living room through to a kitchen, then out to a garden, shortly after Jonny had her undressed and in a jacuzzi, a crowd of people climbed in with her at one point. She woke up alone as a man was getting in. He commented she was naked at that Jonny grabbed her out, covering her with a towel and then got her dressed. She was too drugged by this point to react or do much about it or even care that she was standing there naked in front of a strange man. When usually that wouldn't happen. She walks back to the kitchen and there is standing the host and his two friends, all three of colour, all suited up dressed up. It was a party after all but she wasn't dressed up, she was dragged from another country like she'd been dragged through a hedge backwards. Jonny pointed at Tabitha "she hates black men" then he swiftly walked away leaving her standing there with the three men all staring right at her with shock. She laughed there was nothing else to do at this point, almost spitting out her drink knowing very well she had dated a black man once so why did he say that he was just speaking from his own point of view that was clear but indirectly wanted to get her in trouble. At that the host shouts to "GET HER LADS" before she could turn around they had her and carried her to a big bed in the garden, threw her up on it the two men ripping off her clothes. One of them shouted to burn her clothes on the fire pit or grill. The others agreed as they threw her clothes to onlookers who destroyed her top and bra. The host his name was the Didler shouts, and now for the fisting, i'm keeping on my rings, as he pushed his hand into her she screams and kicks he looks up and orders the two men to hold her legs as she tried to kick him off. One of them shouts and stands on her arms as she is trying to sit up. Her intention was to gouge out his eyes by this point, if she hadn't been drugged and sedated someone would have ended up in hospital. As she's calling out in pain he's ripped her insides with his rings deep wounds which she later got record of at her drs. She looks up one more time and the burly man whos Jonny's wing man grabs the Didler by his shirt collar and pulls him off her and makes the other two men get off her limbs. She goes unconscious for a while, and she's lifted to her feet and he gives her a hoodie to wear to hide her dignity. It wasn't long before she had forgotten the ordeal as that's how a roofie works, and she's back in the kitchen talking to the Didler once more. This time he's trying to be nice. She was glancing around the room and suddenly she spotted a large knife. The only thing in that kitchen apart from glasses and booze was that the place was bare; nobody lived there it was clear. He said firmly "you can take your eyes off that knife right now." She wasn't thinking what he was thinking; she was just wondering why that was the one only thing in the room. It was odd. The Dipper suddenly pipes up "Tabitha. Would you like a tour ?" Of course she responds he said follow me and he does a silly walk round the kitchen island long ways when the door would have been a direct way through but hey how he's odd shes figured or just being facetious. They go through a living room it's dark and she can't see much, "this is where we get the freaky stuff goes down in this room, as they pass through some corridors and come back to the double stair foyer, he once again takes her up the right side of the stairwell when the left side was closer, how odd he was with the directions of choice the short cut would of been her way but oh well this was interesting and she loved the house even though it needed a lot of tlc. They walk up along the landing and he opens the first bedroom door, and there was Jonny in bed with a woman having sex in a missionary style and sat naked next to him was the five year old girl also heavily drugged awake and watching them. Johnny turns to face the door and shouts "A LITTLE PRIVACY PLEASE" as the Dipper closes the door. He begins to turn heel and run back down the stairs, she was trying to process what she just witnessed. Her brain wouldn't react when she saw it but couldn't understand it. The Dipper looks up at her and says you're cool aren't you? She said "yea" already moved on in her mind from what she just witnessed, she hadn't a clue what was happening she felt so odd. He said did you see that he had a child in there, the Didler sounded grossed out by it as Tabitha said what..? He suddenly grabs her hand and walks back up the stairs and along another corridor. In actual fact she can't quite see or remember her way around. If he vanished she'd be lost in that mansion for days. They got to another level and suddenly there was a staircase with a broken balcony, and it made her dizzy. He grabs her hand and almost empathetic caring holds her steady knowing the drop was dangerous on the stairs. She wasn't sure if they went up another level or not but she did see a few bathrooms, one was particularly nice, well it was nice there was plastic wrap all over the vanity unit and it was pulled from the wall clearly about to be removed for sale or replacement. She commented "what a shame, such a beautiful piece, why can't it stay?" There was a big tub in the floor in the middle of this massive room but she wasn't sure if it was a jacuzzi or a giant bath perhaps both. Anyway he said right I'm going back down. "Do you want to go explore if you want?" "Oh no, I'm scared I'll get lost. Can I come back with you?" as they walked back down he mentioned "there are a lot of weirdos here tonight if you're caught alone anything can happen" this is not what you say and this is not a party she's used to. They went back down and his attitude went from nasty to normal but by this point she had forgotten. Suddenly something happened and he was off again. They were standing in the kitchen when suddenly he kicked her twice to the floor in the corner of the room. He orders her to give him back his hoodie and she's shoved in a cab. Just as the driver turns to ask her where Jonny runs and grabs her back, one of the girls gives her a hoodie to wear to cover her dignity. Jonny ; "yea man i'd love to get rid of her but I can't here in this country she needs to come back to the uk with us." He pays the driver and he leaves. Jonny walked her back in and put to bed, but she can't recall going to bed, all she recalls is waking up the next morning the Dipper was asleep on the right, with a grand lavish window on her right as well as the sun shone in, the Dipper woke up jumped up and ran out the room probably wondering who she was just as much as she wondered who he was and by the feels of the damage down below she knew something happened. Jonny walks in hastily " hurry up get cleaned up we gotta go" then suddenly the burly man is standing over her looking at her body as Jonny points out he's done some damage there is already swelling. She walks into the bathroom Jonny follows and he starts having a go at her again for what she didn't know but he was just so moody, probably hung over himself. Then in the walls the burly one comes on and gives her a firm shove but Jonny had upset her but for the life of her she didn't remember why. She blacked out again during the car ride back to the airport and woke up on the plane while off he went again Jonny and his burly man being nasty to her saying horrible things but she was used to it by this point and so drugged up again to make sure she didn't remember any of it. Tabitha just didn't care it was meh, bla bla in her ears. She didn't give a toss what he thought because she hated him by this point.

    The next morning Tabitha wakes up in her own bed wearing the white hoody, it had stripes down the arm and writing on the front, it was a good fit she thought how did she acquire this, then the phone pinged, a text msg, "hey its V, do you remember me from last night?" no as she replied there was nothing more, that was odd who was V? She had to carry on with her day, the children came running into her room throwing their arms around her mummy please don't leave us with them ever again they were so mean to us. I promise I will have words with her, ru ok? Yes mummy we missed you, this was perplexing why did you miss her she hadn't been anywhere, as far as she could recall the night before was the driver dropping her home but she was missing for a few days. After getting the house up and tidy everything was back to normal while there wasn't a single memory to recall of that trip as usual. When she tried to ask the older children what happened they didn't know or have answers so it was brushed aside as nothing, but years later to discover one of Jonny's colleagues was drugging the kids as well keeping them silent while she was trafficked away in and out of her daily life. She had major mental illnesses and was well known by the police but the police were useless in all honestly she kept getting away with things because her solicitor played on her being mentally incapable of knowing right from wrong and she was obsessed with Tabitha. She was the most manipulating evil witch that was a disgrace to all women. The neighbours were asking her where she was for three days. They knocked and heard the kids but nobody answered. They said they heard screaming too, which made no sense at all, thinking he was just nuts but it wasn't until all the lost memory came back that those small conversations made total sense. It's time these people learned how to treat others more kindly, perhaps a spell in prison and counselling would help them but it's highly unlikely now it's been their entire life of dark things, their souls now belonged to the Devil.

Woods and Water

 A long period of time went by before Tabitha thought it was done and dusted when another two murders came back to haunt her. It was a warm month of may back when was a young woman, somehow Jonny had managed to roofie her yet again and this time she woke up in the south of France. She had no idea where she was due to sleeping the entire trip. They pulled up in the car outside a row of quite tall townhouses and outside each front door was a row of concrete shaped boulders along the path. They were facing the opposite side of the road pulled up on the right due to driving on the opposite side which felt odd but she wasn't with it enough to care. Jonny was being extra aggressive this day throwing the odd punches at her for no reason, she wasn't deliberately vexing him she just had it in her naturally to say the wrong thing all the time, and the abuse she wasn't sure half the time what it was this time that triggered him, why he was so hateful to her she just never found out, she never did anything to him except forget him a lot which was beyond her control.   Suddenly the driver jumps back into their car ready to follow another car. Abruptly with aggression she sees the burly bodyguard pulling and pushing a older man in his fifties balding head, being violently shoved out of that doorway of that property, she wasn't sure if it was his home or a workplace, there were shutters on the windows so it was very french period style. While he's being shoved so hard to walk towards his car, holding his shoes in his hand, laces swinging about while he almost trips over running in his socks and doing as he's told. They get in his car which was small in size and drive, and Jonny instructs calmly to his driver to follow slowly behind. Tabitha must have dropped off again to sleep as the next thing she recalls is being woken up along a country road. Trees one side and fields the other. It seems quiet, and pretty. They drive into the field and round a cluster of wooded areas, they all get out of the car and the driver leaves them there. Maybe he was a look out and she can't recall his roll fully. Then the second car gets driven into the middle of the woods. It's surrounded by trees in a circle with an open grass area in the middle but very shady due to all the tall trees surrounding them. So now the car is in place.. She didn't witness the violence the man suffered prior to her being walked closer to the car where the man was sitting on the right hand side and on the other side there were trees so she was standing on the side and the man faced looking ahead which if she turned 90 degrees she'd face the same way as him. He didn't have shoes on it seems he didn't get time to with the rush, he was crying and bargaining with the two men, but to no avail did they show any empathy whatsoever. Then after Jonny shoving Tabitha forward, " look at him hes about to commit suicide." The burly man handed him a red fuel can to tip over himself, being ordered by Jonny and him the man tried to with sobs of tears of fear what he was being made to do. He said I can't because the ceiling is too low, so the burly man poured him pint glasses of fuel, handing them over for him to soak himself in. Tabitha shouted "NO DON'T DO THAT! DON'T BE SILLY" he looked at her "I have to, go, run run, go" he waved his arm with tears down his face let her go, don't bring her into this let her go. Jonny said something in reply but she was starting to feel the effects of the roofie and kept going in and out of it. She watched as he tipped the glass of fuel over himself in so much fear of what was about to happen. It felt like ages but perhaps fifteen min of them saying awful things to him on top of what he being forced to do, just to add torture to what was about to come. She wasn't sure if he was also drugged but for sure coerced into this he definitely didn't want to die and the fact he was trying to think of Tabitha safely meant he was a good man and did not deserve this end. Everyone who ever tried to help her or cause the fall of Jonnys circle ended up dead. She stood there while the others walked backward some feet. She wasn't able to keep herself safe or think in a survival way as she was just about staying up on her feet, eyelids going. She could see him with his right hand trying to light the lighter it didn't want to light, the third man was tall and slim walked around the other side of the open door with a big stick six feet long and jabbed him hard in the left side of his head to push him to hurry up, this knocked him out temporarily and by time he came too there was blood running down over his left eye. Again he was trying to click the lighter, was he drugged or just scared, perhaps both. The burly man walked back around realising he was too weak and threw in a match and up he went… he ran and Tabitha took full blast to the face, the heat made her fall backwards onto the grass. She could hear Jonny ordering his burly servant who just took orders and never really said much, he would just do as he was told.

Ordered to carry Tabitha and pull her back. She came-to outside the wooded area, she had already forgotten what was behind her due to the roofie and how it affects the memory. There was a farmer there now, she wasn't sure if he was the driver or who he was by this stage, everything was a big muddle. The burly man placed her down on her feet, and the three men walked ahead towards a blue car with four doors and a square boot. This time he was pulled up on the left side of the road by the gateway to a dry dusty track going though the field that led from the road to the wood. The farmer looking man had on a wax jacket brown in colour and it had flappy shoulder piece going round the back and it sat on shoulders too round shaped, a weather proof coat. He was tall, he was walking ahead on the left talking to Jonny while the burly man walked ahead on the right leaving Tabitha struggling to walk in the middle of the track left slightly behind. When she suddenly stopped and said holding her arms crossed, "I'm scared" Jonny spouted "why are you scared? We aren't going to hurt you." Still standing there worried faced, she looks slowly left and slowly right, making her way behind the burly man thinking she'll use him as a human shield. "The cows, they are looking at me," they were all just standing chewing grass chilled out totally spaced out and not moving toward her. That was a relief, but their eyes looked right at her and those eyes followed her, they had the biggest horns she had ever seen. Jonny bursts out laughing, "she's afraid of the cows and not us hahahaha," he kept his sense of humour after the horrific thing he just did back there in the woods. Suddenly they hear a scream of horror coming from the black smoke in the trees where the car was burning, Jonny laughed and so did the burly man, "did you hear that?.... there he goes hes still alive,"they made a big joke of his torture. They had a cold heart, and no soul. As they walk around the car Jonny leads her by the arm to the right rear side of the car for her to get in, just as he does so another car comes along, bearing in mind it's a sunny day when the weather will bring out everyone onto the roads. Jonny seems to think daytime murder is the best way to avoid being caught. The car pulls to a stop and a man shouts, something about the fire pointing over to the woods, it was just a field away so close enough to smell it strongly. Jonny piped up " yea man, we wondered that too, I think the farmer was burning something over there, we only stopped so she could have a piss ,women hey." Tabitha blurts out loudly, "NO I

DID NOT!" Jonny, gives her a look to shut the fuck up, and the other car begins to drive off, suddenly Jonny starts laying punches into Tabtiha slamming her into the side of the car. The car suddenly stops and reverses up; he jumps out the left hand side as of course they're in France, and confronts Jonny to stop hitting her. What are you doing, the burly man gets out and challenges him so he leaves. After he's driven off Jonny gives her a few more blows and shoves her into the back seat, where she falls asleep almost immediately, sleep seems to be the only peaceful place while out with them. The three men took her to a hotel, tortuted and raped her. She had no memory of getting home or ever being back in france again from the last time with the tunnel accident, but from what she overheard them chatting about she knew it was linked somehow but by time she was home in bed slept woke there was no longer a memory, it just feels like a nightmare that she would shake away and be grateful that she is at home and not witnessing these terrible events, little did she know they were real. It took decades for her to learn how to cope with the flashbacks of horrific experiences.

By the time a victim remembers, it's often too late. It appears that there's no way to stop the wealthy from breaking laws for which the poor would be punished; unfortunately, money buys freedom. For the plight of innocent victims everyday countless injustices happen and the oppression often through no fault of their own these are stories of the narratives that define our humanity. Innocent victims through all walks of life like children caught in the crossfire of conflict which brings Tabitha to her equally awful event she recalled these two men doing infront of her. One day there must be consequences of violent acts. The trauma inflicted on families.

Jonny had taken Tabitha into a council house where a single mother who was clearly poverty stricken, she had two small children one was a baby, Tabitha was already out of it as they had done the same to her and dragging her along which made no sense why she was always dragged out, but in hindsight, men after a kill need sex and sex is rape goes hand in hand, thats the only form of sex they enjoy it was obvious by this point. The burly man undressed the two babies and placed them into a bathtub half full, the mother shouts to the toddler hold your brother's head up out the water she runs upstairs and Jonny gives her a hard shove he had called her up to him, she lands legs up and head on the floor below the last step. The toddler being drugged has let go of the baby and it submerged, the child looked sedated and had fallen asleep almost immediately still in a sitting position. The mother, unable to get up passes out, and the burly man standing there stopping Tabitha running to the children to help them out of the water , Jonny holding onto her arms from behind "there you go…. that'll do that'll teach her lets go" and dragged Tabitha out the door leaving the tiny baby and a toddler to just drown in a cold no care for children whatsoever way, a heartless callus act of evil. All of the horrors those men committed over decades were allowed to be hidden under the rug. When the woman came she would have woken to one or two children drowning. She would be blamed with no memory of how she was asleep at the bottom of the stairs. How horrific and heartbreaking of an event and evil to take their anger on her out on them helpless small babies.

It's time the law stands up to men who harm children and never let them out, a life sentence should be life forever until they pass away. No more rehabilitation, enough is enough.

We must unite and stand together against violence and injustice where innocent victims no longer suffer in silence and where their rights and dignity are upheld. We have the power to make a difference and it's our moral obligation to do so. As we reflect on these realities we should not only express our sympathy but also commit to action we must advocate for policies that protect the most vulnerable among us. We need to hold accountable those who perpetrate violence and injustice and support initiatives that empower communities, offering education, mental health resources, and avenues for healing. Each victim has a name, a story, and dreams that may never come to fruition.

Chapter Five

~The Match In A Powder Barrel~

Bea had called Tabitha the morning before to tell her she was popping over to visit, she asked could she spend one night because the journey was so distant and catching trains would be a long day to do a day visit. That afternoon she arrived clutching a large over packed suitcase, holding a pair of evening boots and a handbag. "Are you staying one night or a week?" Bea asked and had a little laugh that she really needed to travel lighter. Tabitha had put some little pasties in the oven for them all to snack on, the children included. Bea went into the kitchen and made them with a coffee, Tabitha turned down the oven to as low as it was possible to keep the pasties warm until they fancied them. It wasn't long before Tabitha felt dizzy with a sudden rush of almost passing out. She went to sit in the living room thinking it was anemia as she suffered from this so taking iron was a must. But without being aware she'd been drugged. She wasn't sure how long she was out, nonetheless she woke up unaware of where she was, except she was in Portugal. Bea had stolen her passport and given it to child traffickers. Bea was up to her neck in a sick ring of danger but her mental health was so psychotic she only got off on other people's pain. Tabatha had no idea what day it was, how she got there or any memory of being on a plane, but she saw herself in the newspaper blurred out as an innocent victim. Without recall of events there she didn't act on calling the police, they never help trafficking victims anyway from what she's read up on. Jonny was wearing a fake mystash, Tabitha kept looking at it funny, Jonny would shout "stop looking at it," she'd turn her gaze away but her head was foggy and every ten minutes or so she'd be blank again which was the roofie effect. Jonny walked Tabitha down to a local man's house in a village, all the buildings were white, all the walls seemed solid also white, it was a unusual place to see, it wasn't what Tabitha would call glam but apparently it was popular, Jonny knew a man there but he didn't seem friendly. After they spoke Jonny took her arm and they walked down to the bar. The bar was outdoors, Jonny said wait here I'll go buy you a drink, he looked over at a fair haired lady, "madam would you like a drink?" Before she could reply he'd gone over and bought two beverages and handed them to the ladies. Tabitha wasn't aware she was being kept drugged the entire time, so this was a top up to make sure no memory would surface to unveil their dark secrets of the crime they were about to commit. Shortly after the lady flopped her head down onto the table then sliding her arms under her head she looked all of a sudden incredibly drunk. It was clear she was having trouble lifting her head and seeing clearly. Jonny pipes up " madam would you like this nice lady to help check on your children?" Tabitha looked at him in horror and told him no. The mother lifted her head and firmly said don't go near my children shouting at Jonny with fierce anger. He said ok, grabbing Tabitha by the arm he led her up the hill back toward the van, yet he led her into an apartment where Jonny's two men were both waiting outside, also both of them blond haired, fair skinned, one slim one burly. The burly one shoved Tabitha hard as the big guy forced her into the apartment in front of him. She hit into a crib that startled and woke the children who were sleeping. Jonny came in grabbing her by the shoulders unaware it was his burly pal who'd shoved her into the room. He shoved her into the living room area then told her firmly to stay there by the side board. There was a black stereo on it. She turned around after looking at the furniture which was what always caught her eye in rooms and there standing behind a blue sofa was a man with dark hair, she couldn't understand him. He had a strong accent and being roofied on top she could hardly see or focus. Jonny told him to stay there, waving a gun at him, which looked like a 39mm. He was arguing with the man and it became apparent he was the dad of those children. Being roofied she'd already forgotten being at the bar ten minutes prior so keeping up with what was happening was near impossible. It wasn't until hindsight of flashbacks gathering memory into order she was able to make sense of it. The man shouted pointing at her "I will find and kill you!" Jonny heard the death threat and pointed at her "she's my next victim " that's when the dad started to try and bargain with her. "Will you help me?" Yes depending on what it is if I can yea " "press that button behind you" she turned around and pressed one of the buttons. He explained to find them he needed her finger print. Jonny shouted at her giving her a shove, "don't touch anything" as he used his sleeve to wipe the stereo. He missed the button she touched however she didn't tell him. He walked back to the bedroom and gave orders to drug a child to the burly man. He told the dad you grassed us up, pick one or all die tonight. The father had to make a choice: "take the girl, take the girl!" as he breaks down crying. Tabitha didn't know what the hell was going on and the conversation wasn't making sense in any form. It was so evil and incomprehensible. She felt like she was dreaming, or having a nightmare. The burly man sits the girl in bed and hands her a drink ordering her to drink it, she screams in fear, although she takes it and drinks it in terror. They'd drugged her and before she passed out Jonny shouted through from the other room "come in to say goodbye. " The dad didn't hear him he was pacing back and forth in panic behind the sofa, so Tabitha repeats what Jonny said to tell him, pointing " go say goodbye" she had no idea what she was repeating though, he runs tripping over then to his knees hugs her sobs of tears "I love you goodbye sweetheart" as he walked back toward the other room. "NO," Tabitha shouted to him, waving her arms outright, " don't say goodbye, never say goodbye, say see ya later," that's too final, never say that to your kids!" She hadn't realised what was actually going on she thought they were just going back to the bar and why the hell was she even there for. Suddenly the dad burst into tears back behind the sofa and the burly man came in and a struggle began. He was fighting to keep his little girl but the burly man was too big and overpowered him. He bashed the dad in the nose causing a nosebleed, then he said laughing "don't let dna get anywhere." The burly man had zero empathy or emotional feelings for the situation of those innocent babies in the other room. The third man after being instructed by Jonny to go out the window climbed out as the burly man passed him the now unconscious toddler. He then left via the door while the man carrying the child was up the hill already. Jonny said "right, don't call for the police for another hour or I will put a bullet in each of these babies heads, is that what you want?" he said angrily pointing the gun at the babies, making them scream in terror." The dad runs into the bedroom and shouts in pure grief "look look at that" pointing to the empty bed, now what she's gone she's gone, he collapses in grief sobs of tears. Tabitha had by this point reached her ten min limit where the roofie wiped her and she already didn't understand or know how she got into that apartment. She replied "I don't understand" there was absolutely nothing that made sense at this point. He said " the child's gone from her bed out the window" "What, NO?" she walked to the window thinking what he'd meant was she fell but as she peeked out she sighs "thank god" she was just thinking it's not very high and her mind she was so stupified by the roofie she shouted to the dad who had run in false hope to look out the window himself the child might be there. " Well go find her go look for her " Tabitha shouted in a panic, he shot out the door like a rocket and Jonny came over and punched her why did you tell that for. But the burly man stopped him and he was still being looked out. The third man must have hidden for a while. Jonny takes Tabitha yet again by the arm down towards the bar to look natural and to be seen by witnesses to rule himself out. That's far enough he said as they turned heel and head back up the hill. At this point Jonny points out his mate carrying a child "there he is" ...she was already blank and didn't know who the third man was. Johnny's laughing now gives her a nudge to look at his skin. There was an old man leaning against the building wall looking like he had a major skin rash. It was an illness perhaps not a spot thing. He was now laughing like it was nothing at all to drug and take a child. By the time they got close to the van she was getting heavy and so Jonny carried her but he was angry because someone spotted him. The burly man took her and laid her on a makeshift bench that was locked in by the sliding door. Covered her with a coat. It was pre-prepared, this wasn't opportunistic, they knew the parents, they knew they would be there and had the money to travel to follow them and they knew they would get away with it. The burly man laughing blurted out "she's passed, the drug is too much she passed".. Jonny just didn't seem bothered "oh well he said, so she died then." Tabitha shouted at the burly man, she never knew his name, "don't say that that's sick, it's not funny to joke about death." By this point she hit another blank and had no idea where this child came from. Shortly after Tabitha passes out. She woke to being beaten and raped by the third man, she worked out he was german sounding his accent was thick, she was awake for a few seconds long enough to see the burly man raping the child. As soon as the burly guy realised she'd seen he leaned over and knocked her out. It enraged him for her to see his vile secret; she was supposed to be unconscious but woke briefly. She had woken mid drive. By this time it was dark she leaned in close because she couldn't focus but wanted to check on the child feeling the men were neglecting her, to her relief the girl was breathing but didn't recall the death joke hours before by this point. Shortly after she passes out again and succumbs to the drug and is soon asleep. She's woken by Jonny's laughter, a familiar voice and an old friend who wasn't always insane like this point in time he was now. They must have driven all nt and parked by a woods. Third man as she sits up hearing Jonny joke" you're not going to fuck it are you ?" she looks out and he's carrying something into the woods but too far to see .. Jonny said open that door it stinks in here,it smelt like nappies. She would have had an accident if she's drugged. How is she supposed to use a potty? She wasn't sure how long the third man was gone but he came back and grabbed a rucksack. He grabbed like he was in a bad mood by this point, with a volatile mentality, then headed back into the woods. Jonny orders the burly man to drive round adding he's gone to see his friends. They kept talking in code one minute loud then whispers so it felt like they were just spreading a yarn to distract from the real evil they were doing. She was so drugged she forgot she had a family of her own during the intoxication. No idea how she got in or how she got out of that country the only way she knew she'd been there Jonny always tried to create a fake alibi with photos. She woke in another town unsure how far they'd driven. She was awake for a hr at a time and back unconscious only being allowed to be awake for passing customs but she can't remember that either. Those photos were her only proof. In the third town they stopped in, Jonny stopped a man with similar hair and height, he said "do you want to make some cash waving 50 bucks photo shoot yes ?" the man nodded and he was then handed a beer he was reluctant to drink at first but did. He was now drugged too, another victim who couldn't talk. Jonny took off his own jeans and ordered the man to change into them, he had bought two white T Shirts the same he made Tabitha wear one making the man wear the other. In actual fact Jonny had bought a lot of odd things in town, child and women's swimming costumes. Tabitha must have stank because the weather was hot and she'd not eaten in days or washed. They didn't feed her, only topped her up with more drugged drinks. Jonny was creating a fake holiday scene. Setting up others to look like suspects while he while the burly man stayed off camera. Come on who took the photos. Jonny grabs a random woman and tells her to jump into the van and she's handed a drink but Tabitha can't recall what happened to her or where the child was. She'd forgotten there even was one by this point. Jonny was making a video now of the third man and this stranger woman but Tabitha didn't understand what language they spoke. Imagine having that gift of being bilingual and not being a normal person using that in a job but decide being a criminal is a better option … not so intelligent perhaps. But to be that clever and not use talent for good seems such a waste. Tabitha wakes up and Jonny is trying to order the drugged man to rape her, she can't open her eyes but hears no no no. By the time she's awake again she'd already forgotten it all. She accidentally wakes up a little girl who was asleep, she'd forgotten who she was and the rapes the night before. As the child sits up she reaches down holding her groin in pain then her tummy screams in pain.. as a third man shouts and hits her to shut up Tabitha sees red shouts at him presuming he's her dad as she's a blank again… "don't speak to her that way. And don't hit her or I'll hit you see how you like it," she was mad. Tanitha grabs the girl and says I'm going to take you to your mummy and the girl seemed comforted and she knew she was safe with her. Both of them were dizzy. She got no further than twenty steps. Tabitha begged a stranger to help "help, call the police! " she felt she needed to find a policeman but the stranger waved a 'no' plus he didn't understand her different languages. She was suddenly grabbed from her arms by Jonny and dragged her back to the van," you think you're gonna live after that attempt you can't escape." They shoved the child after handing her more drugged drink under the bed on the floor. Tabitha came too again unaware if she was knocked out, choked out or drugged. Jonny told the stranger who he drugged and used for a fake photosboot to fuck off hitting him, the man didn't speak enough English but he looked horrified he fell to his knees trying to rush away from another blow, as Jonny threw the money to the floor as he scrambled to grab it Jonny shouts angrily "keep the jeans with your shitty ass and smelly ballsack." He didn't want them back. The man had a lucky escape unless the burly man raped him it wouldn't be a shocker as he was like that. Her next memory is of them walking up a steep hill in the woods. They moan how hot it was but joking like it's a normal day taking kidnapping in their stride. The code they talked in wasn't hard to crack. They kept saying the girl was dead. They had a large rucksack they all kept joking about and how Tabitha won't need to worry she's not walking back down with us but she was to die with the girl. All this danger went over her head. They came to a river, the third man stripped off and while Jonny undressed Tabitha and pushed her in ..it was the only way to freshen up where they didn't allow her to wash or eat. In fact the third man did sneak her half a sandwich but when she complained about its flavor he soon snapped with threats, the sandwich was prawn, it smelled very strongly making her stomach turn but she was starving so ate it fast so not to be caught by the other two men. The German was a very volatile man that had no control over their mood swings. Jonny was still taking photos and videos by this point it was clear they were to set the German up as they were all him mostly. Placing him in that country when the girl was taken. Jonny really set him up, that's clear. Suddenly Jonny and a burly man throw the rucksack into the river, "one two three" they laugh, it lands about six feet out and starts to sink slowly. Burly man wades in, dragged it out half way and it's waist deep he flips into a mental episode and starts punching the rucksack then rage is laughter, then rage again as he pushes it under. He then clenches his fists growling now I kill you he shouted to Tabitha. Johnny shouts " do you want to die are you ready to die?" She looks at Jonny and feels a blow to her head and she's underwater. Her next memory is on top of a high view spot in the city where they're being spiteful and cruel. Photos taken. That's how she recalls and places memory's in order..photos help with cued recall, they didn't before but now she has learned how to process these memories. She had forgotten everything that was behind her right up to the very start cooking at home. The girl didn't exist in her memory anymore but now in the future she realised she almost escaped with her. She almost lived up to her promise of taking her home to her mummy who she was calling for upon waking. That now resigns heartbreak for what they did to that innocent child. No child should pay for their parents' mistakes. It's pure evil to do that.. how can Jonny pretend to love his kids and kill other people with no remorse. The man back in that village where she was taken from was he who told them where she was. Who told them they'd be there, why do it on a holiday none of made any sense. The dad must have reported the traffickers and that was his payment. But they kept lying about her being dead so she had no way of knowing if she was still under the seat and the bag stuffed with clothes. Tabitha was woken outside the third man's home, it looked like it could have potential, she could hear Jonny shouting grab a bag full leave the rest, you're never coming back you got to run now. We have 3000 miles to go back the other direction he spouts. She just went back to sleep. She had zero recall of yet how she got there but Jonny made her sit up, look to the right and say this is Germany. She soon passed out. They drugged her so much she was getting weak. She'd lost half a stone easily in those few days. She's been nudged again however this time they're going round the back of some old tatty deserted industrial site. There was another car and the man in it she'd seen before with Jonny on his bus to Ireland and Cirencester, but she didn't know his name he was also burly short with an unhinged childish temper in the same way as the others..like the raging tantrums of toddlers in full grown men who had no control over themselves. Not a great combination. The underdeveloped mental capacity to control their emotions. They walk her into an old deserted factory filled with rubbish where she wrote her name on the wall. German told her to so when she haunts it they can read it. Jonny whispers " this is the last place you'll see on earth now you die." They sat her in a corner, held her down, placed a cloth over her face and waterboarded her. Asking her over and over about the little girl's name. Do you know her? Do you know her? She couldn't reply. They didn't give her time to breathe so taking a breath was the first choice and questions ignored. Then a burly man poured petrol over her, saying " smell that you're going to die now."- Before they could light her up a man came in, the young man from the other car they knew him he was in it too and a older man..he acted like what are doing in here… but Tabitha had listened to their act they weren't good at acting, it was just lie after lie after lie. They stood her up, walked her to an open area and Jonny gave orders to tip paint all over the fuel to pretend to clean up paint with petrol ..but he wasn't convincing. They washed her off with a cold water hose when the Cirencester man shouted "let's kill Tabitha." He was grinning so much but she was distracted by the burly man dropping an object into a well making a loud slash. He was grinning ear to ear as you'd expect a mental institution patient to look during an episode. He said you weren't supposed to see that. But she didn't click. She hears whispering then cries of pain but again it felt like an act. Jonny is standing beside her telling her she stinks again

.. (I mean der..) in that moment she feels her body convulsions begin the same way when she stopped breathing years before. Her blood pressure dropped so low they weren't feeding her or giving her water for days and her body begins to fit before she passes out..the last thing she hears is Jonny saying concerned quick go grab, as the cirencester man spouted, he cares about her I knew he cared about her, … she didn't hear what he said next. She woke at home with no memory of travelling..the day Bea arrived she had been cleaning all day but the morning she woke her home.was filthy . Her bathtub was oily (from the petrol) she accused her guest of using a bath bomb. She spent that day cleaning again and didn't realise the large suitcase was a big clue she overlooked. She left soon as Tabitha was awake. The kids didn't say a word so she was never sure if Bea had been drugging and abusing her kids while she was human trafficked. Bea had now officially been part of a murder investigation. The news came on and she'd heard a horror story about a kidnapping but all she could think was why if she had been missing since Sunday is she only hearing this days later. The memory's wiped like a bad dream and stored in the pile with nightmares. There was nowhere to turn now and nothing she could do. In hindsight was the child in a river, in a well, or trafficked to them men from cirencester? It was comprehensible they kept lying about her being dead. But to live in hope to return her to her mummy It's heartbreaking. She had several places in her mind about where the child could be but she has no memory of her being dead. She recalls a pre dug large grave they told her she and the child will be buried in, she recalls the two burly men shoving soil into the hole in the woods. But weeks later there was a memory of being in a sports centre, her and the child were shivering in a changing room, the smell of chlorine, the child shaking fiercely perhaps the cold pool or the drug wearing off as she was now awake, but Jonny is standing close watching so they can't escape, suddenly he gets a phone call, he hushes his burly pal standing nearby, waving his finger over his lips, a deal is made and shortly after the child's mother comes grabs her and thanks Tabitha for returning the child. This memory is the most perplexing, she overheard Jonny say, now keep her hidden well ok, the mother nods. She walks away clutching her child close in her arms. Was this a wishful thinking of a happy ending, was this fraud? One thing is for sure if it was money related, did the father do the right thing, the only way he could, pleading for his baby back offering millions of pounds to be laundered to Jonny for her freedom and her life. A father will do what it takes to save his child, that's real love, money means nothing to a loving parent as long as they have that child safe , that's all that matters. All the odd little signs your body tells you is instinct .. listen to that because it's never wrong. Tabitha prays she's found safe and back with her family one day, but hoping she's been there all along. During the time of recalling events these men have attacked Tabitha four more times that she recalls so far, even breaking into properties to grab her. To also raping her child by gunpoint and threatening if you tell the police all your kids will be killed. They follow her more than not which is perplexing as she's an old Lady now. What really is his obsession with Tabitha ? She will never fully understand if he hates her that much why just not stay away and avoid her. She's not bothering him or following him so why is he following her?

During these trafficking trips, he had taken her all around the world, New York, the Caribbean Islands to a private island owned by his billionaire friend who was murdered in prison for his sex trafficking in the end they were caught, but she was there she experienced the horrors, the only good part was they locked her in a straw hut in the heat but it was a break from them. Jonny sent a burly man who had privately told her he didn't like hurting her. He was under orders from Jonny that had Sumat on him so he would force him to do things for him. He walked her back to the huts along the pier, they looked like luxury beach huts sitting over the sea, there was a building on a pier that was for entertainment, a bar and a kitchen where Jonny made it clear while she was sleeping on the hot sand they had partied all night in the air con building. He walked her through into a kitchen, he laughed and pointed out a naked baby sitting in a sink which was clear it was the same sink in the room she was standing in. The owner of the Island had his wife standing behind him, he spoke up, if my wife wasn't here i'd have some fun with you, this made Tabitha's stomach turn, she was thankful his wife was there. She had no idea they were all swingers. Suddenly he popped up saying, "Shall we eat her" he laughed, as Tabitha grimaced. Jonny suddenly piped up, he was standing close behind her holding her shoulders walking her around showing her things. " no we can't eat her she's not pure she would be vile to eat shes full of toxins." well he was forcing them on her all week. When the news came on TV decades later of all these men who had a history of abusing her, suddenly it was like a memory cue as things slotted into place. He showed her around some unusual rooms like nothing she'd seen before, thankfully it wasn't long before they had to grab a lift back to a scruffy looking building to fly home. The island wasn't as impressive after all, they lived their lives just like a real life horror movie. Tabitha couldn't recall how she managed to get home but photos she found in the news made it crystal clear she was on the right track.

The end
Synopsis

This book The Nefarious written by the Author Mia Collins is the fifth sequel to the Sangfroid series. As the story unfolds the narrative becomes clearer in each episode as the truth evolves, one memory at a time revolving for decades, amnesia, a unravelling sinister turn of untoward events during Tabitha's enigmatic life. A long overdue divide of opinions will shake you to your core. The similarity of events unfolding in this fictional story was created to sound like a familiar event to further the philosophy to give a window into how the felonious get away with crimes, these aren't your run of the mill misdemeanours, but a jinxed one might say; when bad things happen to Tabitha you can guarantee karma will equal the balance of bad luck to the indictable offence. This proverbial book series will have you talking and questioning the adherence of crimes for years to come. Readers will be squirming with grimace, disapproving of the pain caused, but moreover will be restless for karma to reach the offenders for these conundrums of events, and crimes they get away with. Verdict being as a result_ Tabitha's wrath would shake the world and watch it rattle. Illustrations created by the Author. Sketches illustrate fake people. Triggering warning: This addresses themes of human trafficking, exploitation, and abuse. The content may be distressing and could evoke strong emotional responses. Stories have been depicted for narrative effect. The story being an alleged theory about how some crimes may perhaps have panned out diversely to how the media expressed.

Printed in Great Britain
by Amazon

b536f54e-095d-49a8-bfd2-30334682bc15R01